*Rico wanted to marry her.* For real. "Why?"

"Because I want a son. An heir."

Sick disappointment churned in Danielle's stomach. "You misled me. Deliberately. Do you know how much that really pains me?"

"Pain?" He spoke so softly she strained to hear him. "I know about real pain. And all because of your father."

"I can't give you a real marriage."

"Because you're a Sinclair? A princess? And I'm a peasant?"

"No, I don't want to marry anyone because—"

She froze as he placed his hands on the sofa back, trapping her between his arms, and lowered his face to hers. "You're *going* to give me a son in exchange for all I've lost at the hands of your family."

Dear Reader,

*Rich Man's Revenge* was a book that was an absolute delight to write. Rico D'Alessio is this macho Italian guy who wants revenge at all costs, but Danielle Sinclair is more than a match for him and succeeds in surprising him at every turn.

From the first moment I started hearing Danielle and Rico sparring with one another, the book just flowed. Not that it was all plain sailing, because the two of them have some pretty thorny issues to work through. But it's really satisfying to see how they went about solving problems that sometimes seemed insurmountable to me, their creator.

The manuscript went on to final in several contests, among them The Golden Heart Contest and The Emma Darcy Award. I was thrilled that readers had loved the story enough to score it highly in such prestigious contests. As a finalist for an Emma Darcy Award I got to spend time with Emma Darcy herself and discuss my story with her. It was one of the highpoints in my writing career. For so many years I had read and enjoyed Emma Darcy's Harlequin Presents books and now *she* was talking to *me* about my story.... I can tell you, it's the stuff that dreams are made of!

If you'd like to find out more about the stories behind *Rich Man's Revenge* or about my upcoming releases, please come visit me at www.tessaradley.com.

*Tessa Radley*

# TESSA RADLEY

# RICH MAN'S REVENGE

Published by Silhouette Books
**America's Publisher of Contemporary Romance**

SILHOUETTE BOOKS
®

ISBN-13: 978-0-373-76806-6
ISBN-10:  0-373-76806-0

RICH MAN'S REVENGE

Visit Silhouette Books at www.eHarlequin.com

**Printed in U.S.A.**

**Books by Tessa Radley**

Silhouette Desire

*Black Widow Bride* #1794
*Rich Man's Revenge* #1806

## TESSA RADLEY

loves traveling, reading and watching the world around her. As a teen Tessa wanted to be an intrepid foreign correspondent. But after completing a bachelor of arts and marrying her sweetheart, she became fascinated with law and ended up studying further and practicing as an attorney in a city practice.

A six-month break traveling through Australia with her family re-awoke the yen to write. And life as a writer suits her perfectly; traveling and reading count as research and as for analyzing the world...well, she can think "what if" all day long. When she's not reading, traveling or thinking about writing she's spending time with her husband, her two sons—or her zany and wonderful friends. You can contact Tessa through her Web site www.tessaradley.com.

To contest judges and coordinators everywhere. These hardworking people taught me so much and opened doors to opportunities I might never otherwise have had.

A big thank-you to Helen Kirkman for convincing me that *Rich Man's Revenge* would sell— your belief spurred me on.

Thanks also go to Karen Solem and Melissa Jeglinski for invaluable input and advice.

Thanks forever to Tony, Alex and Andrew— you guys are the greatest—true heroes.

And, as always, thanks to Karina Bliss, Abby Gaines and Sandra Hyde cheerleaders, kick-in-the-pantsers, comedy act and critique partners supreme! Check them out at www.novelchicks.com.

# One

It was done.

Danielle Sinclair let out the breath she'd unconsciously been holding all day and thrust the snowy bridal bouquet of lilies, freesias and baby's breath into a hand-blown glass vase on her dressing table. Kim was safely married. At last.

After years spent looking out for her sister, dragging her out of endless scrapes, Kim was no longer her problem. Kim had a husband—and Danielle could relax.

The wedding of the year had been an ornate, A-list occasion frothing with white lace, formal flower arrangements and French champagne. Not exactly what Danielle had expected of her wild-child sister. Yet Kim had glowed in a stylishly un-Kim designer gown, her fiery hair framing her willful—yet unexpectedly pale—face.

As the festivities had drawn to a close, Kim had turned, scanned the crowd, then flung the bouquet straight into

Danielle's unsuspecting arms. Clutching the blooms and enveloped with their heady perfume, Danielle had stood statue still. Catching a bouquet was not going to land her a groom—and certainly not the man of her dreams. If life had been that easy she'd have done exactly what Kim had done—spent wedding after wedding clawing like an agile cat at tumbling flowers, until it brought her the man she'd sought.

Danielle only hoped Bradley Lester, the CEO of her father's company and her newly acquired brother-in-law, knew what he'd let himself in for. But Kim deserved a slice of happiness—after the humiliation and misery Rico D'Alessio had put her through four years ago.

No. She wasn't thinking about *that man* on Kim's special day. He could burn in hell for all she cared! Danielle glanced at her wafer-thin gold watch. By now Kim and Bradley should be comfortably ensconced in the Hilton's Premier King suite overlooking the luxurious superyachts berthed in Auckland's Viaduct Basin. Tomorrow they'd fly out for a slice of tropical heaven in Fiji.

Danielle unpinned her hair and gave her aching head a shake. Oh, bliss. A swathe of mouse-mixed-with-toffee whispered across her shoulders. The pins tinkled from her fingers into the dresser drawer, and she nudged the drawer shut with her knee before shimmying out of the tight magenta taffeta sheath she'd worn all day. Out of habit she hooked the dress onto a hanger—even though she'd never wear it again.

The deep, rich colour wasn't her choice. She'd have gone for a cool aqua or an elegant iced blue. But who argued with a bride? Especially one everyone wanted to see settled.

A quick bath to soak away the aches from the too-high shoes and the forced, social smile she'd worn all day, and then she'd see what her father wanted to talk about. Perhaps she'd even get a chance to look over the report she'd finalised yesterday before she went to bed.

Work was something she understood far better than weddings.

"What the devil do you want, D'Alessio?"

*To take you and your daughter to hell with me.* But instead of declaring his intent, Rico D'Alessio ignored Robert Sinclair's demand and towered over the wide desk that would've dwarfed an ordinary room. Here, in the immense space of Sinclair's study in the Paritai Drive mansion, the desk barely filled a corner. With scarcely a glance at the splendour surrounding him, Rico slowly and deliberately placed the knuckles of his clenched fists on the antique desk and glared at the man on the other side.

Rico had to give Sinclair credit. The older man didn't cower in the face of six foot three of taut muscle. Nor did he quiver as the sole heir to countless generations of hot Italian D'Alessio blood leaned further forward.

Then Sinclair blinked.

So his former mentor *was* nervous. Rico narrowed his gaze as Sinclair glanced past him to check that the minions were in place. Rico wasn't particularly worried by the presence of David Matthews, Sinco's top legal eagle. Nor was he concerned about the young bit of muscle packing a gun who stood beside Matthews shivering like a whippet ready for action. But the dark, thick-set man across the room was another story. Ken Pascal would be the man to watch.

The glimmer of sweat beading Sinclair's brow gave Rico intense satisfaction. Sinclair was going to sweat a lot more before this was over.

"I told you on the telephone yesterday that I'd compensate you." Robert Sinclair gestured to a pile of paperwork in a wooden tray at the edge of the vast desk. "Sign the contract David Matthews has prepared and I'll arrange for a lump sum to be transferred to an account—anywhere in the world."

Rico clenched his jaw. "No sum of money you pay me could make up for what I've lost."

A frown creased Robert Sinclair's brow. "So what do you want?"

Rico decided to go for broke. "Everything!"

"Everything?" For the first time the other man looked disconcerted. "What do you mean, everything?"

Sinclair was good, damned good. But good wouldn't be enough. Only a couple of days after receiving the call from his lawyer, Rico had flown to stand by his ailing father's bedside and endured his plea for a grandson. Later the same day, in a cemetery on the outskirts of Milan, his heart swelling with pain and unforgotten grief, Rico had sworn revenge. On Lucia's grave. For the first time in four years he had a mission: to return to New Zealand and make Robert Sinclair and his daughter pay. Already one of his goals had been thwarted: Kim was married.

Rico gave Sinclair a slow, menacing smile, allowing it to widen as the first hint of naked fear darkened the older man's steel-grey eyes. "You have a problem understanding the word *everything?*" Rico asked, his tone softly mocking. "Perhaps we can find a dictionary that can define the word?" He arched a black eyebrow. "Or it's my accent, hmm, that you are not able to understand?"

Sinclair set his chin pugnaciously. "Your English is impeccable, D'Alessio. How could it be anything else—after a decade in New Zealand?"

Rico shifted onto the balls of his feet, the desire to punch the other man rising through him. With effort he restrained himself. He had no intention of getting himself arrested. Even though he didn't give a damn about much anymore. "So what exactly is it that you do not understand?" he murmured, and gave Sinclair a reckless, don't-care smile for good measure.

More tiny droplets of sweat sprang out across the other man's brow. "What do you want?"

"I want my shares in Sinco Security returned and compensation for what I've lost."

"Done." Relief made Sinclair's voice gruff.

"And I want more."

"How much?" Sinclair looked at Rico as if he resembled something nasty and scaly that had crawled out from under a log. Rico curled his fists, fighting the fury and pain that threatened to make him run mad. So Sinclair still thought he could be bought! Rico's lip curled. Robert Sinclair's wealth had once lured him like the vision of a mirage to a thirsty explorer. Now he no longer needed Robert Sinclair or Sinco Security. He possessed a fortune beyond Sinclair's wildest dreams.

A fortune he hadn't wanted for the price he'd paid.

But Sinclair didn't know that. Sinclair thought he was dealing with a rootless wanderer he'd driven into exile. Through tight lips, Rico said, "I don't want your bloody money."

"So what do you want, D'Alessio?" Sinclair fired the staccato words at him.

If Sinclair only knew…

Rico thought for an instant, floundering to find the words he might have used four years ago, before he lost all respect for the man opposite. The answer came in an instant. He met Sinclair's shrewd metallic eyes. "I want my place on the Sinco board back." He deserved it—he'd worked his guts out to help build Sinco Security into what it was today. It had been he who had come up with the idea of providing supersecurity to the wealthy making Sinco a force to be reckoned with in the Australasian-Pacific region. "And, damn it, I don't just want any position, I want to be CEO."

"Impossible—that position is already filled." Deep lines snaked across the older man's forehead. "Come on, D'Alessio. I'm a reasonable man and I'm trying my utmost to accommodate you."

Abruptly Rico stood and headed for the door.

"Where are you going?" Sinclair sounded alarmed.

Rico swung around and raked a lean hand through his hair, his fingers smoothing the overlong locks into an illusion of order. "To get some photos taken. There'll be a high demand for them in the morning papers. Oh, and perhaps I'll call some television channels. See who'll make the best offer." He threw Sinclair a careless smile. "Ciao—for now."

Of course, he had no intention of selling his story to the tabloids. But Sinclair didn't know that. As Rico turned toward the door, he could hear Sinclair grinding his teeth. Satisfaction curled through Rico when Sinclair spoke from behind him. "Don't be so hasty, D'Alessio."

Rico stopped dead and swivelled on his heel, insolence loaded into every move. No doubt Sinclair had never had to beg in his life before.

But he'd learn.


Later, bathed and dressed, all the professionally applied makeup carefully cleansed away, the gooey hairspray and mousse washed out of her hair, Danielle felt refreshed and relaxed enough to turn her mind to her father. Robert Sinclair was a man who thought of little but work. After returning home, instead of celebrating Kim's wedding over a glass of champagne with his remaining daughter, he'd tersely told Danielle he wanted to see her in an hour in his study.

A frown furrowing her brow, Danielle smoothed the crinkle

cotton fabric of the white dress she'd donned. She was late. Twenty minutes late. And her father hated being kept waiting. But for once she took pleasure in dallying, a hint of unaccustomed rebellion stirring inside her.

Kim had always been the wild one. Several years ago Danielle had tried to escape the prison the beautiful mansion had become, but her father had blocked every attempt she'd made to move out to a flat with old school friends. Eventually her girlfriends had given up on her, pursued their own lives, leaving her behind, still living with Daddy.

Danielle grimaced. How incredibly stupid she'd been—not paying attention to how isolated she'd become. There'd been her degree to complete—plus the unremitting pressure from her father to attain top marks.

And, of course, she'd also had her hands full with Kim painting Auckland red, ricocheting from one crisis to the next, while Danielle damage-controlled behind her, hiding the worst of her sister's high jinxes, wheedling with Kim's minders not to report her sister's excesses. How much her father knew she couldn't tell. More than she suspected, no doubt—because he'd used Kim as another hold over her.

She'd been the submissive daughter for so long, it had become habit.

Even as she made her way to the door of her suite, the shrill ring of the phone stopped her in her tracks. That would be her father, ordering her to hurry. Resentment warred with the urge to obey. For three shrill rings she considered ignoring the summons, then the ingrained habits of a lifetime kicked in and, with a sigh, she crossed the thick cream carpet to answer it.

"Kim?" Danielle failed to hide her astonishment as her sister's voice greeted her. "What's wrong?"

Kim was babbling. "Try not to hate me. I couldn't live with

it all hanging over me. Not when I was so happy. I had to do something."

*Oh, no.* "Whoa, slow down." Danielle tried desperately to make sense of the fractured statements. "What have you done?" She bit back the damning *this time*.

Silence. Then, "Hasn't Daddy told you yet?"

"Told me?" A longer, more ominous silence. Danielle took a deep, calming breath and counted to three. "No. He's called some sort of meeting, but wanted to see me first. I should go. I'm already late."

"He's going to tell you." The jagged sound of her sister's gasp came over the line, causing Danielle more concern. "Danielle…I'm sorry."

"About what?"

"Daddy will tell you." The phone clicked.

"Kim…?" Danielle called desperately.

But the line had gone dead.

Danielle set the handset down, the relaxing calm from a soak in fragrant bubbles evaporating like hope before a raging fire.

"I read that you'd gone into kidnap retrieval."

Rico turned to meet the level scrutiny of Ken Pascal, Sinco's chief of security. "Yes. I did."

The three words didn't reveal the horror and atrocities he'd witnessed over the past four years spent in Iraq, Afghanistan and Africa. Flying to trouble-torn hotspots into situations that appeared hopeless to negotiate some poor bastard's release. He was good at it. Together with Morgan Tate and Carlos Carreras he'd set up a corporation to train task forces and private security contractors to deal with kidnap threats, a corporation which his two partners now ran—and in the process the three of them had made a great deal of money.

"What does that have to do with anything, Ken?" Sinclair asked impatiently.

"It's a good opportunity to get into that game, boss. Rico can see if it would be viable for us to look at—or perhaps there are other fields where he can see opportunities for Sinco."

"I'm not heading up a special-projects unit," Rico said flatly.

Sinclair tilted his head. "It would give me a chance to talk to Bradley about resigning as CEO."

Rico felt a thrill of victory. He nodded at the telephone on the desk. "Get Bradley—" he drew out the name contemptuously "—on the line now."

"I'm afraid that's not possible. He got married today," Sinclair said tightly.

"Of course, I'd forgotten. I read about it in the papers. Boss's Daughter to Marry Sinco CEO. Good news for both families—and the shareholders, hmm?"

The other man looked wary. But he remained silent.

"Of course I have…how do you say—" mockingly Rico let his subtle Italian accent become more pronounced "—unfinished business with the bride."

"You know, boss, he may be exactly what we need."

Rico turned his head and assessed Ken Pascal through slitted eyes. Had the passage of time scrambled the man's brains? Pascal had never been stupid. And the one thing everyone in the room knew was that Robert Sinclair needed Rico D'Alessio like a bullet to the brain.

"Look at him. No man's going to mess with that," Pascal was saying. "Not unless he's totally beyond reason."

Sinclair appeared to know what Pascal was on about, Rico realised, not liking the measuring way his broad shoulders and bulging arms were being looked over. As if he were a piece of prime horseflesh that the man was considering buying.

"What exactly would you need me for? Some dirty laundry that needs sorting? Driving another good man into exile?"

Pascal coughed. "Danielle Sinclair needs someone to watch over her."

A vision of Sinclair's earnest eldest daughter leaped into Rico's mind. Young, quiet and very, very troubled. He pushed the memory away.

"What about a bodyguard?" Rico asked. "They're not in short supply around here. Or did the last one get caught nicking the family silver? Or maybe the lady tried to get into his pants, hmm?"

Every man in the room gasped at his insolence. This time Rico flung his head back and laughed out loud. Laughter, he'd learned, was a useful tool to conceal the tormenting rage that spurred him on, ever closer to destruction.

"I don't want D'Alessio near my daughter," Sinclair said flatly, his face pale. "He's insane."

Rico laughed again.

Pascal's eyes flickered. Addressing Rico, he said, "Danielle has refused all offers of help. She's as stubborn as her old man." Then he turned to Sinclair. "Robert, if you don't do something fast you're not going to have a daughter for much longer. I tell you, Rico's the answer."

"Won't have a daughter for much longer?" Rico asked. "I can't believe she's running out on Daddy. Where's she going?"

"Six foot under, if the psycho stalking her isn't apprehended." Pascal crossed to the desk and picked up a large manila envelope and a cloth. "May I?" He looked to Sinclair for permission.

Robert Sinclair's shoulders slumped as he nodded.

Rico took the cloth and envelope from Ken Pascal and glanced inside. Slowly he pulled out a single photo, careful not to leave fingerprints or wipe any that might already exist.

His eyes widened in shock, then narrowed in outrage.

It was a picture of a wedding. Today's wedding. His mouth flattened as he recognised the bride, Kimberly Sinclair. The vibrant face he remembered wore a sedate smile as she stood between her father and a man who had to be Bradley Lester given the goofy look on his face. But it was the fourth figure in the photo that made his breath catch.

The slender body was clad in a clinging dress of some sort of dark pink fabric—the kind of pink only a worldly, passionate woman would dare wear. If this was Danielle Sinclair then she had grown up. But it was her face that drew his attention—or what little had been left of it on the photo after being slashed with a deadly blade.

Rico stared at the mutilated photo, his heart pounding. Pascal was right. She needed someone to watch over her before she landed stretched out and stone cold on a mortuary gurney.

And he hadn't held her hand through the worst time in her life just to let some lunatic hurt her.

The instant Danielle pushed open the door to her father's study she sensed the tension. It hung over the room thicker than a pall of smoke. Her eyes landed on the broad shoulders of the unknown man who *had* to be the cause. He stood with his back to her, his legs slightly apart, his body angled so that his left hip confronted the four men ranged before him. Despite being outnumbered, she had no doubt he was in total control.

A brief glance confirmed she knew all the others. Her father, looking frustrated; Ken, her father's chief of security, appeared a little calmer; while David, her father's trusted advisor, wore the poker face he adopted when he was desperately searching for a solution to some complex conundrum. The young security guy whom Ken had singled out as a man to watch, Ty? Tymon? Tyrone?—she'd forgotten his name—was clearly out of his depth.

Her gaze returned to the stranger. The other four men watched him as they might a dangerous animal, their wariness apparent in the way they stood, out of reach and careful to face him. She wanted—no, needed—to see this man's face, read his eyes, understand what made him a man among men.

Danielle blinked to dispel his powerful image, but couldn't help a last appreciative glance to take in the way his shoulders stretched the black T-shirt, and how the black denims—so new that the creases still showed—clung to his behind and long legs. He was only a man, she told herself. Albeit a finely built one. But she couldn't prevent her eyes tracking slowly upward over his taut rear, his lean back.

He was holding a file—no, an envelope and something else. An instant later he turned. Her heart stopped at the first glimpse of his hard, dark profile, and hot confusion swept her as he swung to face her. Something flared in the depths of his eyes as he recognised her, then a shutter came down and he shoved whatever he'd been looking at into the envelope and set it down. Her blood started to pound, hard enough to make her head ache.

*Rico D'Alessio.*

Cold fury clutched her heart, but she kept her gaze level, not wanting to show the hatred the name, the man, engendered. Heck, she'd even been admiring his body. Her stomach heaved. She sucked in air, striving to pull her usual serenity around her like an all-concealing cloak.

"What's this all about, Dad? Why is he back? What does he want?" She whirled around, searching each face for answers, waiting for someone to take charge…to hurl him out of here. "And why haven't you called the police?"

"The matter won't be pursued," her father said reluctantly.
"Why?"

Rico D'Alessio's gaze clashed with hers. He looked arro-
gantly amused…and something else. Danielle studied the
curve of his sensual mouth, the glitter of his black eyes.

He was angry. Beneath the carefully arranged amusement,
he was absolutely bloody furious.

What did he have to be so mad about? He was the bastard
who'd harmed her sister. Why was he here? In their home. Vio-
lating her family. Again.

Bewildered, she looked back at her father. "I need to call
Kim." To warn her sister…and to get out of this oppressive
room.

For a moment her father looked old. "Kim already knows,
she's the reason he's back. She changed her statement."

Danielle gasped. Her head spun and she felt oddly dizzy.

"Sit down, Danielle." She barely heard her father speak.

*How could this be?* When Rico D'Alessio had left the
country four years ago, she'd been so relieved. Known he'd
never hurt Kim again. And now he was back, filled with a
deadly intensity that was a world apart from the man she remembered.

*Oh, God.*

"Sit, girl, before you faint."

Mindlessly she obeyed her father's impatient command
and sank down opposite him.

An instant later the cushion beside her subsided beneath the
force of a far larger, heavier body. She turned her head and
silently met the dangerous gaze of Rico D'Alessio.

# Two

"Princess, don't tell me you thought I was guilty?" Rico challenged Danielle Sinclair, watching her through narrowed eyes. He couldn't—wouldn't—accept that she'd been as ignorant as her wide-eyed shock suggested.

Hell, forget shock. She looked shattered.

"Of all the people in the world, I'd have thought *you'd* know how I'd react if I was confronted by my employer's daughter bent on seduction. And rape wouldn't be it." He spoke softly so that her father, seated across the expanse of the priceless Persian, couldn't hear, and his body shielded her from the others.

"You weren't accused of rape." But she'd paled, and dainty white teeth closed on her bottom lip.

He dropped his gaze to her mouth and heat rushed to the junction at the top of his thighs. Rico shifted. This was a trap he hadn't expected. For an instant he wondered if she still wore the lacy white panties she'd tried to tempt him with all those years ago. He took in the feminine white dress she wore, nothing like the pink sheath she'd worn in the photo.

He tore his attention from the pristine dress, the fine-boned, slender body beneath, and, careful to hide his unwanted reaction to her femininity, met her eyes.

The grey-green depths were raw with turbulence; her confusion bringing out an urge to protect. The response disturbed him. It had been a long time since anything—anyone—had stirred him. "Robotic" was how Morgan and Carlos, his business partners, referred to his lack of emotion. Could this response be a holdover from the sympathy he'd felt for her after her mother's death? She'd been so damn brave.

"No," he agreed. "I wasn't accused of rape. But only because your father trumped up a charge that would stick more easily. Tell me, *do* you believe I seduced your sister? Or as the police put it 'had unlawful sexual connection with a minor'?"

Confusion clouded her eyes. "I don't know."

"Not good enough!" For some reason he needed to hear her say she believed him, that she'd never suspected him of the repulsive accusation.

"So Kim lied?" Her voice lifted, making it a question rather than a statement.

Damn! She *had* thought him capable of harming her sister, of betraying the trust that went with being her father's protégé, his business partner. Anger gnawed at him but he said nothing. He'd learned—the hard way—that sometimes saying less was better.

Finally, when the silence grew unbearable, he glanced at Robert Sinclair and raised his voice, "I'd suggest you get those guys—" he hooked a thumb over his shoulder "—out of here."

"Danielle has known Ken and David all her life. They came

to her christening for God's sake," Sinclair said with an arrogance that made Rico's fists curl.

Danielle shifted beside him. "Daddy, could you ask them to go? Please?"

Her soft, breathy voice sounded as if she was near the end of her tether. Rico hadn't expected the sympathy that seeped through him. It clashed with the rage that had buoyed him for the past ten days since his lawyer's call.

Her father shrugged. "I don't see what the fuss is about."

"I think your daughter would like a little privacy to come to terms with what she's discovered," Rico said as coolly as the fury bubbling inside him allowed, then wondered why he was defending her.

Sinclair rose and crossed to where the rest of the men huddled.

From beside him Danielle spoke, "I want you to go, too."

Rico glared at her. "Not a chance…Princess."

The taunt rankled. The stiff way she held her body told him that. When the door thudded shut behind the departing men, Rico almost wished he had gone because she cupped her face in her hands and her shoulders began to shake.

He glanced desperately around. Hell, what was he supposed to do now? He *hated* it when women cried. And Danielle cried silently, he remembered. She'd wept for her mother during the long hours after the accident. At the funeral there'd been one final bout of weeping, and after that…nothing. Sure her eyes had been sad for a long time, but he'd never seen another tear. Unlike Kimberly, who'd gone through huge dramatic upheavals necessitating long spells of therapy. And Kimberly hadn't even been involved in the car accident that had killed Rose Sinclair, nor had she been trapped inside for the two hours it had taken the emergency services to cut Danielle free. Awkwardly he patted her shoulder. His thumb touched the bare skin at the top of her arm. It was soft and silky. With a guilty start he withdrew his hand.

"Why did Kim do it?"

Her voice was so faint that he leaned closer. He'd wondered, too, and four years on he was no closer to a conclusion. Unless it was the old hell-hath-no-fury thing.

"Who knows? Perhaps she was having a bad hair day."

Danielle didn't smile. Instead she folded her hands in her lap withdrawing further into herself. "You never…touched… Kim?" she whispered, her grey-green eyes huge in her white face.

"Remember what I said that night in my defence?" His mouth twisted at the memory. "I had a wife. A wife I loved, who was going to have our baby. Why would I've screwed that up?"

She frowned, her face uncertain, puzzled. "But later you left—"

"I wasn't given much choice, was I?" he said bitterly, glaring at her.

She glanced down, her hands twisting in the white fabric of her dress. Mercilessly he watched her throat move. "I'm sorry. I heard your wife died."

"'I'm sorry' doesn't cut it," he said harshly. "It won't bring Lucia back."

Her head jerked at his brutal words, and for an instant he felt remorse. Danielle knew about the pain of losing a loved one. She was the last person he should be taking his anger out on. For a heartbeat his resolve crumbled, then he steeled himself.

*She was a Sinclair.* She'd been a part of it all…and she was available. A frown creased his forehead as he started to think about that. Kim might be married, but her sister was not.

"You hate us," she was saying. "You really hate us. So why are you here?"

"Your family owes me." The look he gave her wasn't meant to be kind.

"You want revenge?"

She was quick. And she was straight. He'd always liked those qualities about her. "Let's say I want to be recompensed for what I lost." His lips twisted. That had to be the understatement of the century.

"Oh." A strangely disappointed expression flitted over her face. "You want money."

*No, Princess. There are many things I want, but money isn't one of them.*

But he didn't say that. Instead he gave her a slow smile. "You're fast." The sucking sound of a door opening and a cool draft on the back of his neck made him swivel. Sinclair was standing in the doorway with Pascal behind him. Rico turned back to Danielle.

She was staring at her father. "He's been saying—"

"You used to call me Rico," he interrupted, speaking softly so that only she could hear.

Colour surged into her cheeks. She raised her chin a fraction. "D'Alessio's been telling me that you've got to compensate him. Has this all been resolved?"

"We're ironing out the finer details." Sinclair gave her an absent smile. "No need to worry yourself about it."

Watching the flush deepen on her honeyed skin, Rico decided the man might as well have slapped her down publicly and told her not to worry her pretty little head about petty things like money and injustice. He found he wanted to distract her from the patronising put-down, to clear the hurt from those lake-grey eyes. "I get a position on the Sinco board, too."

She turned to him, her eyes shadowed. "What position?"

He hadn't made up his mind until that moment. But now

he knew what he was going to do. It was so simple, he couldn't believe he hadn't thought of it before. "Princess, I'm in charge of special projects."

"What are you doing here? This is Martin's office." It was early on Monday morning. The Sinco offices were usually still empty at this hour and Danielle certainly hadn't expected to be confronted by the tall, dark man seated at her boss's desk.

"I believe the esteemed human resources director is at a conference in Sydney this week." Rico didn't even look up from the sheaf of papers he was studying. "And when he gets back he's off on paternity leave. The builders have to do some rearrangement on the tenth floor where I'll be housed, so I'm here for now."

*I don't want you here.* Danielle bit her lip. It sounded so childish. Yet it was true. Separated from her office only by the alcove of space occupied by Cynthia, the secretary she and Martin Dunstan shared, Rico was far too close for comfort. "You can't work here."

That brought his head up.

"Surely it's no big deal?"

His voice was tinged with impatience. Danielle looked down at her knotted hands and shifted restlessly from foot to foot. It shouldn't be a big deal. How could she explain how over-whelmed she felt? She couldn't. Because she couldn't explain *why* she felt that way. Not to him. And not even to herself.

"I want to show you something." Rico held an envelope in his hands. Propelled by curiosity, she moved forward. "I don't believe you should be kept in the dark like a child." His fingers brushed hers as he passed her the envelope. "Open it."

Feeling a little like Pandora, Danielle lifted the flap. Her breath caught as she stared at the photo, the vicious incisions where her image had been.

Distantly she heard Rico say, "I'm no profiler, but whoever he is, I'd say he means business."

Danielle couldn't think of anything to say that would lessen the terror that tore through her. A finger jabbed past her, landing on the massacred photo. "That's why Pascal and your father are worried. That's why I'm in the office next door."

She swallowed, choked a little. Why did it take something like this to get her father to notice her existence? Instead of blurting that out, she raised her eyes and said, "Why you?"

"Because you refused a bodyguard."

Oh, God. "I don't want you—"

He rocked back in the leather chair. "Why not?"

"Because…" She struggled to find the right words.

*Because I don't want you near me all hours of the day and night.* Especially now that she knew Rico was no longer married, wasn't guilty of terrible treachery against her sister. What had Kim been thinking of, making such an accusation? And she couldn't even ask her sister until she returned from her honeymoon because she wanted to see her sister's eyes when she confronted her, watch them widen or flicker, to test whether her sister's responses were the truth or more lies.

But deep in her heart she believed Rico. There was no other explanation for his fury, for her sister's revocation.

*Try not to hate me. I couldn't live with it all hanging over me. Not when I was so happy. I had to do something.* Kim's haunted words made sense.

The Sinclairs *had* betrayed Rico.

But despite her pity for his predicament, she didn't want him near her all day long. "I don't need a minder," she said truculently, glaring down at him.

He tilted the chair back. "I'd say the photo proves you do. But have it your way. If you don't want a bodyguard you get me."

*"I don't want you."*

"Why not?" His eyes were too sharp.

She felt herself flushing. "I don't trust you."

He went white.

Oh, God! He thought she meant…

"No, not for that reason." Kim had cleared him of that. "I don't trust you because you want payback. Do you really think I'm going to be stupid enough to give you an opening to find ways of leveraging it higher?"

"Do you blame me?" He looked away. The silence lengthened. At last he said with quiet ferocity, "I *need* the board position in Sinco."

Danielle's heart sank. He'd lost so much already at her family's hands.

He must've sensed her distress because he spoke quickly, flushing slightly. "This board position will give me a start— a chance to regroup—gain back my reputation. Once your father appoints me CEO he even gets to keep his monetary compensation and the interest he offered."

"Poor Bradley, he's in for a shock." She smiled sadly. "But so are you. My father's not going to let you dictate the terms."

The dark eyes that met hers were expressionless. "Oh, yes he will, Princess. I can do whatever I like."

She gave him an incredulous look, saw that he was deadly serious and started to laugh, torn between hysteria and disbelief. "He doesn't know what he's got."

He raised an eyebrow.

"My father has a twenty-four-karat tiger by the tail, and he doesn't have a clue." She almost laughed again. Here was someone her father could not control. She could hardly wait to witness Robert Sinclair's frustration.

Rico held his hand out for the photo, then dropped it back into the envelope. "Just remember I'm not your bodyguard. You need to take care. I have a job that's going to take most of my time and attention. I'm only keeping a very part-time eye on you because Pascal and your father are worried about your safety. Your father already has to deal with me. This way he gets to kill two birds with one stone—give me a toehold into Sinco without having to oust Bradley yet, and frighten off this parasite at the same time. Simple."

"You think you'll frighten him off?"

"Well, your father and Pascal certainly think I'm frightening."

Danielle assessed the grim smile that slashed his face, the tall hard body, and wasn't surprised that he'd put the fear of death into grown men.

He frightened her, too.

D'Alessio was dangerous. Far more dangerous than some screwball sending her hate mail. And her father and Ken were entrusting him with keeping an eye on her.

She sighed. "Okay. You can stay. Not that I ever had much choice."

The tension in his shoulders gave a little. "I'll be taking you home. And starting tomorrow I'll be picking you up from your father's home each morning."

Danielle bit down on the unfamiliar urge to curse a blue streak. But her aching heart wouldn't let her forget the odd note in his voice when he'd insisted that he needed this position at Sinco.

The rest of the week proved to be uneventful. Danielle was irked at how seamlessly Rico fitted into her daily routine, how easily he adapted to the hum and bustle at Sinco's headquarters. She had far more trouble adjusting to his presence next door while she tried to work. To be honest, she'd gotten little done. Every time he spoke, the hint of accent that belonged only to Rico seeped into her office breaking her concentration.

On Friday morning she clenched her hands around the

steering wheel and decided she couldn't afford to let Rico scramble her brains; her work was too important to her. Danielle slowed as the traffic light ahead turned red. Stopping, she yanked the hand brake up hard, then turned her head to glance at the man beside her. "Ready for another hard day at the office?"

She'd been astonished when he'd arrived at her father's home on Tuesday morning and hadn't automatically commandeered the keys to her zippy BMW convertible the way her father did when he drove anywhere with her; her overcautious handling of the sports car drove him wild, even though everyone knew her caution around vehicles came from painful experience.

Rico's only comment—after critically surveying the sparkling white vehicle with its folded-down roof—had been that from now on the top stayed up.

As they waited for the lights to change, he smiled at her, his teeth white and even. "You certainly put in the hours. What are you trying to do? Win the Employee of the Year Award?"

There was no such honour at Sinco. But it wasn't a bad idea. In her capacity as human relations team leader she could implement it. "Maybe."

"Don't bother."

Startled, she looked at him. "You don't think I'd get it?"

"No."

Chagrin filled her at his certainty. "I happen to work damn hard! I graduated top of my class at business school, and I've been fast-tracked on the Sinco management program. And I assure you it's not because I'm the boss's daughter."

"I believe you. Nothing to do with your abilities—but you won't get it."

"Why on earth not?"

"Because you're not a man." His eyes were shaded by the annoyingly dark lenses that hid his expression.

Very sexy. Very Italian. She wrenched her attention back to the road…and to the topic they'd been discussing before his sexiness had distracted her.

"You think my father's a chauvinist?"

"Of course he is!"

Unfortunately Rico was right. Her father had little time for women in the workplace—or on the board. "And you're not?" She sneaked another sideways look, which he intercepted.

"I like women." He smiled, a slow smile that made her heart tremble.

Danielle drew a shuddering breath. She couldn't allow the sinful attraction Rico had always held to mess with her brains. "I'm sure you do!"

"The lights have changed." His tone was gentle.

"Thanks for the reminder," she said tartly, and let out the clutch. Too fast. The car jerked and stalled. She didn't dare look at him, or at the long line of cars in the rearview mirror. Instead she bit back a curse and restarted the car, then pulled smartly into the stream of traffic heading for the city.

Once settled in her office, Danielle opened her e-mail program and started to go through the unread messages, pausing as she came to a message from an unknown e-mail address. It didn't look like spam or a virus. "Urgent memorandum," the subject line read. She glanced at the body where the text usually was. Nothing. Frowning, she opened a drawer and reached for a disk. Quickly she saved the attachment to the disk and ran it through the virus software. It was clean.

She clicked…and screamed.

Focused on the awful image on the screen, Danielle barely heard the running footsteps. Instead she stared at the face atop the body mutilated beyond reason. *Her face.* Shudders of horror and shock quaked through her. Distantly she heard Martin Dunstan say, "What happened?" as he came toward her.

The next instant Rico erupted into the room. "Get down, Danielle. On the floor. Now." She obeyed, sliding under the desk and covering her eyes with her hands in an attempt to block out the images.

"You," she heard Rico's voice, hard as gunmetal, "Get against the wall."

"But—"

"Don't argue. Just do it."

"You don't understand—"

"No, mate, you don't understand. Against the wall. Now."

"Jesus, that's a knife." Martin's frantic words caused Danielle to raise her head.

"Yeah, that's right. Now face the wall and put your hands up above you."

Danielle slithered out of the space beneath her desk. Her eyes widened at the sight of Rico leaning over Martin. From the stiffness of Martin's back she could sense his terror as Rico patted him down. In the doorway Cynthia was shifting indecisively from foot to foot, a hand over her mouth. Danielle stepped away from the desk. "Rico, Martin's no threat."

Rico grunted, finished checking him over—she assumed for weapons—and stepped back. "This is Dunstan?"

Danielle bit her lip. "Er, yes…that's Martin Dunstan, my boss."

Rico frowned at him. "You look different from your security photo. Where's the beard? And aren't you supposed to be in Sydney?"

"I shaved it off." Martin rubbed his clean-shaven jaw. "I caught an earlier flight. My wife is due to have our baby any day. I'm sorry."

Rico swivelled to face her. "You screamed." His eyes were colder and darker than she'd ever seen them. Like black ice.

Danielle shivered.

"Why?" Already he was prowling around her office, eyes snapping, Martin forgotten.

She didn't need to answer.

Two paces took him to her computer. He stared at the graphics without flinching, his big body motionless. Then he reached for her phone. Danielle tried to feel irritated at the way he'd taken over, but she couldn't summon the energy. For once it was a relief to have someone to lean on. She looked at his broad shoulders, thought about resting her head against his solid chest, and sighed.

He had her in a flat-out spin.

# Three

Several hours later, after the police had been and gone, Rico insisted on taking Danielle home. Despite her objections that she had work to do, her relief was clearly visible.

Rico couldn't understand his compulsion to stay close to her side during the barrage of questions from the police, and even less comprehensible was the tangle of emotions he'd experienced: fear, rage and a curious need to shield Danielle from the world. Morgan and Carlos would laugh themselves silly to see him now. No resemblance to an automaton remained.

And it terrified him that he was starting to feel again, that the attack on Danielle Sinclair had become personal.

He'd shooed away the curious onlookers who kept visiting the sixth floor. While both Ken Pascal and David Matthews had turned up, Robert Sinclair was conspicuous by his absence. The information that Sinclair was too busy finalising security arrangements for some top-brass delegation from the United States to come offer his daughter support caused Rico to seethe. And despite Pascal's constant calls to update his boss, Sinclair still hadn't spoken to his daughter.

The hurt and bewilderment in Danielle's eyes enraged Rico. At least he'd been there for her, he thought as he ushered her into the elevator. Robert Sinclair didn't deserve a daughter like Danielle.

"Now you understand why you should treat this guy seriously," Rico growled ten minutes later as Danielle whipped the BMW along Tamaki Drive, a different route from the one they'd taken to the city this morning—by Rico's insistence.

The tide was in, and the midday sun had transformed the sea in Hobson Bay into sparkling bright-blue diamonds. There wasn't a cloud to mar the azure sky. Normally Danielle would've pulled over and wound the roof down, but given her fright earlier, she suspected it would be a while before she felt secure enough to ride in an open car.

And that enraged her.

"Okay." She shrugged. "So you were right. But I still don't need you on my back 24/7."

"Princess—" the word stroked her senses, and she forgot how much she hated it when he called her that "—you should be so lucky."

She flushed at the subtle, sexy tone, and pressed her foot down on the accelerator, the unaccustomed need for speed surprising her.

"Hey, slow down!"

She threw him a challenging glance. "Scared?" she taunted, determined to flee the sensual images that terrified the wits out of her. Almost as much as she feared having a madman watching her. But no one was going to drive her into some dark hole where fear ruled her. On second thought, she'd rather play the dangerous game of challenging Rico's machismo. "I was surprised a man as tough as you let me drive my own car," she cooed, and batted her eyelashes outrageously as she stopped behind a line of congested traffic.

She heard him snort. "The only reason I didn't drive was because this way it left my hands free to find my weapon."

She shot him a provocative glance. "You keep your hands on your weapon all the time?"

He stared straight ahead, not responding, but Danielle swore the flush along his cheekbones hadn't been there before.

"And there I thought you respected my right to drive my own car." She clicked her tongue. "Does being driven by a woman frighten you?"

He shrugged. "What Italian man would pass up the opportunity to be driven around in a sports car by a beautiful blonde?"

She glared at him, but inside her heart sang. *Rico thought she was beautiful.* Suddenly the day brightened and the sky turned bluer.

But she had to set him straight. "I'm hardly blonde, more like mouse."

He sputtered. "Princess, if you're a mouse, then the cats better watch out."

For the first time in three hours the dark void that trapped her started to recede, and, unable to help herself, Danielle broke into laughter.

When they returned to the white mansion on Paritai Drive she headed for her suite of rooms, Rico hard on her heels. Danielle wanted nothing more than to change out of her business suit and sink into a bath full of bubbles to cleanse away her earlier fright. But with Rico breathing down her neck, intent on not letting her out of his sight, the bath was fast becoming a dream.

Unless she could shake him off.

She took a deep breath, opened the door to her rooms and said, "Stop right there."

He barely slowed. "I want to check that everything is secure," he said, brushing past her and causing her pulse to go haywire.

She caught his hard arm. She wasn't going to allow another man to browbeat her. "I've lived here all my life. Believe me, it'll be fine."

"Humour me, Princess. Okay?"

His lips kinked into a smile that immediately caused her pulse rate to pick up. She swallowed at the unexpected warmth in his eyes. Heck, she'd withstood his intimidation, but she had no defence against his charm.

"Wait here."

Danielle started to argue, but one look at his rocklike jaw dissuaded her.

He was back in seconds, his brows drawn into an uncompromising line. "Out!"

"What—"

"Trust me, you don't want to go in there."

She pushed past him, but even in her hurry to force her way past, every nerve cell that made contact with the tensile strength of his body went on red alert. Ignoring the heat that flared through her, she burst into her sitting room. Rico grabbed her shoulders from behind, and another shaft of hot awareness pierced her.

"Danielle, you don't want to do this."

She wrenched away, but his hands tightened on her shoulders. "It's *my* life," she snapped. "I have a right to see what you're trying to hide from me. I'm an adult, Rico. And I'm tired of all the decisions being made for me like I'm some doll."

He sighed. "Okay. I've told you before I don't believe in treating you like a child, but I didn't think you needed this. Not on top of everything that has happened today. Are you sure you're up to another shock?"

Her throat tightened. Anxiety mixed with something close to determination, and she nodded. "I'm sure."

He released her shoulders and gave her a gentle push. "In the bedroom. But don't say I didn't warn you."

She rushed toward her bedroom and came to a standstill at the threshold. Chilled, she stared at the previously white bedcover. Smears of red—blood? she wondered frantically—had been viciously and arbitrarily splattered across the white-on-white embroidered cover. The overpowering scent of bruised freesias hung like a pall over the room. In the centre of the double bed, amidst broken flowers torn from the bouquet she'd caught—was it only five days ago?—lay Annabelle, maimed, her face crushed.

Blindly, she ran to the bed, set on picking Annabelle up, cradling her, trying to make the hurt better like she had for years after her mother had given her the precious doll.

"Leave it!"

She jerked to a standstill at Rico's harsh voice.

"The police will need to see the room untouched." His tone softened as he stopped in front of her. His hands closed around her upper arms and Danielle stifled a dry sob.

*Her bedroom was a crime scene.*

"You need better protection. This guy is showing he can get to you. I don't like it."

Danielle blinked. "What can I do?" she asked, intensely aware of the press of his fingers against her arms. "I don't want a bodyguard. I can't live like that."

Rico hesitated, his eyes half-closed. Another shiver shook her at the dark glitter of cool calculation. Then it vanished and he became Rico again.

"You could marry me."

Stunned, she gazed up at him. "Marry you? You have to be joking! *Why?*"

"No joke. I'd be with you all the time, you'll never be alone at his mercy."

Instead she'd be at Rico's mercy! But in lieu of dread, the thought sent a secret thrill shooting through her—as heady as her first glass of champagne. She gazed through lowered lashes at the firm, full mouth that had been the focus of countless daydreams when she'd been seventeen. That mouth and his husky voice had aroused desires that she hadn't known how to go about fulfilling—desires that had embarrassed her. But she'd had no one to ask about the hot and cold shivers Rico had caused within her, the restlessness he'd stirred. And the only person she could've asked had been dead.

And now her teen idol was proposing marriage to her. Her world tilted on its axis. Roughly she shook loose of his hold. Rico let her go. She took a step back and contrarily wished he hadn't released her.

*Mum, what do I do?*

Her mother couldn't help her, no more than she could've years ago after all the pent-up longing had boiled into that fiasco when she'd thrown herself at Rico.

Just the memory made her blanch. Rico and her father had planned to spend a weekend brainstorming future plans for Sinco Security. On the Friday night they'd been closeted in her father's study and she'd spent the evening pacing to and fro listening to the deep cadence of Rico's voice as they'd worked late into the night. Boy, she'd had it bad.

The meeting had eventually broken up well after midnight. Danielle's heart had been knocking at her throat when she'd rapped on the door of the guest bedroom Rico had been given.

He'd opened the door, lost his smile when he saw that she wore only a sheer robe with satin insets, her feet bare. Frowning, he'd demanded to know what she wanted.

She'd rushed past him and, forgetting the words she'd prepared—romantic words, words of utter adoration—she'd dropped the robe and looked at him with her heart in her eyes, naked but for a pair of skimpy lace panties.

There'd been no loverlike response. Rico had been furious. Yelling that she was little more than a child and he was a man with a wife, he'd ordered her to get out. She'd wanted to *die* of shame. To find a place where she could hide her head for a hundred years, and never meet his eyes again.

But she'd forced herself to face him, to meet his remote gaze, no longer filled with sympathy and gentle humour…to grab the robe and run from the room. The next day he'd been different—withdrawn, his eyes remote.

And now he was asking her to marry him.

"Marry me, I'll make everything right, you'll see." His voice was hard with certainty. She looked into his glittering eyes and her heart shifted in her chest.

Could he make everything right? Desperately her eyes searched his. No longer the same eyes she remembered. But he'd offered her a chance. She could marry him, get to know the man he was now. Discover whether his relentless gaze hid the gentleness he'd once shown her.

She bit her lip. She wanted much more than tenderness…she wanted to know what it felt like to have Rico touch her…kiss her. Danielle glanced furtively at his lips, now drawn into a hard line, and imagined them pressed against her own. Heck, she'd used fantasise about that all the time. But she'd been a teenager, with a teenager's dazed romanticism, she suspected the kind of adult kiss she craved would be a world apart from her naive contemplation.

Her lip stung. Abruptly she touched the spot where she'd bitten too hard.

"It's too late," she said, knowing it was true and wishing the knowledge didn't hurt so much. Far better to put a stop to this now, before she lost her head. Hadn't she decided to forfeit the whole marriage dream? To pursue her studies instead of guys like most of the girls at university?

"Marriage isn't necessary," she added, her voice cool and remote. She swallowed. There would be no kissing Rico, no learning whether he tasted as dark and forbidden as he looked.

"Okay, so what about a pretend marriage?"

*"A pretend marriage?"* She heard the incredulity in her tone, and felt a moment's relief at his persistence.

"Why not?" Rico moved closer. "A very public pretend marriage. Think about it. The story will hit the papers. He'll be intimidated and go away once he realises you've got a man, that you're no longer available. Or it will drive him crazy, make him do something reckless. Then I'll get him." From the gleam in his eyes Danielle saw Rico relished the thought. "Either way you win…you'll be safe again."

It made a weird kind of sense. But still she hesitated, searching for a logical reason why it wouldn't work. "My father wouldn't allow it…even if it was only a hoax. My wishes don't count for anything. Nothing matters to him except money…and control."

"Your father doesn't want you dead."

*He'll never let me go*, she wanted to retort. Yet she held back. Because Rico was offering her a way out. All she needed to do was say yes.

Staring into those dark chocolate eyes, she didn't blink, dared not let her gaze move over him, in case he saw the yearning in her eyes. Because he was offering all her dreams and fantasies in one package. A chance to be free of her father's domination…and perhaps…perhaps even…

Her heart started to pound. Oh, God, she didn't dare think about *that*.

"A pretend marriage. God knows what my father is going to say." Nerves balled in her stomach at the thought of telling her father.

"So don't tell him. It's your life. Tell him it's real. He won't have a choice," Rico snarled.

"I can't do that. I find it difficult to stand up to him." It sounded so feeble. "I won't lie to him."

"So do something about reclaiming your life. Change your job, get a flat. You don't have to live under his thumb."

She stared at Rico.

He might as well have said, *Get a life*. How could she explain that she'd tried to move out before, to escape the oppressive control her father held over everything around her? Only to be thwarted every time. And then there'd been the rewards for staying, the promotions at work—even the appointment to charitable trusts that her father controlled, to positions her mother had once occupied. The subtle pressure, the endless guilt, had ensured that leaving became impossible.

But Rico was talking again. "Your father won't argue. By agreeing to this sham marriage, he gets to whitewash the wrong he did me. A lot of people think me guilty of a crime I never committed." Danielle coloured and looked away, guilt gnawing at her. "He's astute enough to understand that—and it will cost him much less than the face he'll lose if I proceed with legal action against Kimberly."

Would he ever forgive her for doubting him? "I'm so sorry, Rico." Sorry I didn't believe in you more, sorry I didn't doubt Kim. *She hadn't thought about what Rico might get out of their pretend marriage*—the chance to be seen at her side, to clear his name irrefutably. He wasn't suggesting a pretend marriage only to keep her safe. It would be to his advantage as well. The knowledge made her feel easier.

Her hand brushed his before she was aware of reaching out. "Believe me, I hate the thought of people thinking you were guilty of something you didn't do."

His hand fisted under hers, then slowly his fingers uncurled and he turned his hand over so that their palms met. Something jerked inside her. Then his fingers linked through hers, and a rush of emotion swept her. A memory rose of a time she'd clung to his hand, when the hold of his fingers around hers was all that stopped her sinking into a vortex of anguish.

Now Rico needed her. To clear his reputation. He'd lost so much; she'd be forfeiting so little. How could she refuse?

His fingers squeezed hers, and she looked up. "Don't worry about your father. Marrying me makes perfect sense. Pascal and I will convince your father."

"Thank you." She gave him a smile, deeply relieved that he'd offered to deal with Robert Sinclair, while a little voice sing-songed *Scaredy-cat*. "You're my hero."

At her words his eyes burned, black and dark, and a quiver of heat shook her. Oh, God, they weren't even married yet, and she couldn't control her response to him. Did he intend…?

"We won't have to share my suite, will we?" she blurted out.

The flame in his eyes went out, leaving his expression inscrutable, his eyes dark slits that showed no colour, no emotion, and his hand slid out from under hers. But high on his cheekbone a muscle moved. "We'll be sharing more than a suite, we'll be sharing this bedroom, I want to be there when he tries to get in again."

*"When?"* Unease quaked through her at his certainty. Danielle glanced around her bedroom. The suite of rooms

that had been hers since her thirteenth birthday had always seemed spacious and far from cosy. But suddenly the space had shrunk. She folded her arms and hugged herself tightly. The thought of Rico in her bedroom all night was deeply disturbing. "Don't you mean *if?*"

"Definitely *when*. I don't think he'll give up easily. And it must look like we share a room. We don't know what access he has to information about you."

"You mean someone is feeding him snippets on what I do, where I go?" Danielle felt violated.

"You can't discount it. How else did he get into your bedroom?"

Suddenly Danielle no longer felt safe. A desperate need to get out of the familiar walls that were closing in on her overwhelmed her. The red-stained bed made her want to get out of here and never come back.

"I'm never going to sleep in that bed again," she resolved, glaring at it.

"Get rid of it. Buy another," Rico said.

He was right. It was that simple. She started to relax and uncrossed her arms. "I think I will. What will happen to Annabelle?"

"The police will probably take her."

Danielle closed her eyes against the image of the smashed face and broken body. For so long the doll been her closest memory of Mum. Poor Annabelle.

She eyed Rico. "I don't want to stay here…not after this." She gestured to the bed. "I couldn't sleep in this room again… not even on a new bed."

"What about moving to Kimberly's suite?" he asked, sounding cautious.

"No." She drew a deep breath. "If I do this—pretend to marry you—I want something out of it, too."

"Like what?" Rico asked, his eyes suddenly sharp.

"Freedom," she said succinctly. "You're the one who calls me princess. I need to escape the ivory tower, live somewhere else. Somewhere where I'm not under my father's control."

Suddenly Rico didn't look at all happy. "You're safer here. The security is top class."

"It doesn't look like it, does it?" She lifted her chin, refusing to back down. "Those are my terms, move out or no pretend marriage. Take them or leave them."

He gave a disbelieving snort. "Princess, you're hardly in a position to negotiate."

"I know, but I'm giving it my best shot."

A harsh sigh escaped him. "Okay. You can come stay in the apartment I've temporarily rented. The security isn't bad, and I'll talk to the landlord about adding a little extra."

"No! I'm not moving out of here into another man's domain. That's too much like jumping out of the frying pan into the fire. I want somewhere that will be mine. All mine," she emphasised, the vision becoming more concrete with every word. A home. Her home. Somewhere she could place her stamp on, no interior decorators, just her. "This way, when this charade is over, I'll have my independence at least." It would almost be worth being stalked and living with Rico as pretend man and wife—despite her misgivings—for that freedom.

Taking advantage of the fact that he was listening and hadn't discounted her comments, she pointed out, "You can secure the place I find. At least you won't have to worry about breaches of security by staff or about any knowledge this madman has. He'll have to start his reconnaissance afresh."

Rico held her gaze for a long, tense moment. She could hardly believe her relief when he finally nodded. "Done."

# Four

The following Saturday Danielle stared at the convincing-looking priest at the altar and felt nothing but disbelief...and a curious numbness.

The actor Rico had produced looked like an authentic Catholic priest. Even the ceremony had felt real from the moment the fine veil had been peeled back from her face and she'd looked into Rico's hooded eyes.

The masses of scented white flowers, the heart-rending vows Rico had repeated in a deep voice as he'd stood shoulder to shoulder beside her in a pale-grey suit looking utterly devastating, did little to reinforce that this wedding was nothing more than an ornate performance. Even the slim-fitting pearly sheath she wore, the bouquet of tiny white roses she carried were what Danielle would have chosen for the wedding of her dreams. The wedding that she'd convinced herself could never happen. After all, what man would want her, after she told him—

"You may now kiss the bride," the priest's—no, actor's—voice interrupted.

Danielle stiffened as panic swept her. Hadn't Rico instructed the guy to remove this bit from the ceremony? She didn't want to kiss him. Not in front of two hundred people who'd been hurriedly invited to give credence to her bogus wedding—not that the guests knew that, of course.

Rico's head angled towards hers. Danielle considered shutting her eyes before deciding she needed all her senses on wide alert.

The touch of his lips was gentle, resting for an infinitesimal second against hers. For a fleeting moment she thought that the welcome numbness enshrouding her would negate his impact. But something imperceptible changed, her mouth softened, his breath caught…and her heart started to pound. Her eyelashes fluttered down as a tingling heat stirred deep within her.

Then the moment was gone, and Rico was stepping back. She sighed and her shoulders sagged. With relief that the kiss ended so quickly? Or longing that he hadn't kissed her with the passion she suspected him capable of?

"Almost over," he murmured. "Then you can relax."

Relax? She suppressed a nervous giggle. When in a couple of hours she and Rico would be closeted in the bridal suite and tomorrow they'd move into the cosy town house she'd bought four days ago? For the first time she was having second thoughts about the wisdom of living alone with him. At least in her father's house they would've been constantly surrounded by people.

A quick, sideways glance revealed his harsh profile, his raven-dark hair spilling onto his forehead, his jutting nose and his generous lips.

Shivers of excitement mixed with apprehension danced

over her bare shoulders, then raced down her spine at the thought of those lips brushing her skin. Her hand involuntarily tightened on his arm. He turned his head, his eyes wary.

She swallowed and gave him a weak smile, hoping he didn't detect the frisson that pierced her as their eyes met. After a moment he smiled back but without a hint of the raw sensuality she craved.

She could breathe again. Rico had absolutely no idea how much he got to her.

Had always gotten to her. Words from the service washed over her and shame curled through her. After her mother's death she'd been so desperately in need of comfort that she'd imagined herself in love with the man whose hand she'd clung to through a terrible time. She'd believed that the shared experience and pain would bind them together. Forever.

But it hadn't been love. She'd been infatuated with a married man who'd proved his lack of interest when she'd thrown herself at him by his brutal and unequivocal refusal of her blatant offer. Rico hadn't been interested back then, and he certainly wouldn't be interested now. Not with all that the Sinclairs had put him through.

Then he was tugging her along with him in the wake of the academy-award-deserving priest to an adjacent chamber to sign a fake register, and to smile for the cameraman her father had arranged.

As they began the long walk back down the aisle, the sound of organ music swelled through the church and Danielle's heart clenched. The smiling faces in the pews blended into a haze and for an instant she wished hopelessly that all this was real, not some expensive sham she'd entered to catch a killer, but a *real* marriage.

The wish shattered as she and Rico stepped out of the church into the fresh air. Danielle blinked then flinched as the bright summer sunshine and the noise of the baying reporters hit her simultaneously. Rico ushered her rapidly along, his arm hard around her shoulders, while the press surged forward against barriers heavily patrolled by Sinco Security employees.

She could feel the tension winding Rico's body tight as he pulled her close against him, screening her with his larger body, providing protection from whatever threat lay out in the crowd. The gesture caused a burst of warmth and affection to flood her.

A black Bentley pulled up, and Rico opened the door. At least now she knew what it felt like to be a bride. He'd been everything a woman could hope for—and more. He'd played the adoring bridegroom without fault, like a pro. Of course, he was hardly an amateur. He'd stood before an altar before. Except, his first marriage had been based on love. It certainly hadn't been an elaborate ploy designed to lure a madman into the open.

Deftly Rico manoeuvred her into the waiting car, driven by a Sinco driver she recognised through the separating glass as Bob Harvey, a man her father had sent on several offensive driving courses. She'd never cared much for the man, disliking the way his eyes roved over her and his overfamiliar manner. But today he sat staring firmly ahead, clearly unwilling to tangle with Rico.

Once the car was moving, Rico's intent gaze met hers. "You made a beautiful bride."

"Thank you." Danielle felt like a Christmas tree that had been lit up, bright and sparkling. Lips curving, she let her eyes skim his elegantly clad body. "You don't look too bad yourself."

He shifted, looking uncomfortable. "The wedding day belongs to the bride."

"This is hardly a real wedding," she felt compelled to remind him.

Immediately Rico shot a warning glance in the driver's direction.

Danielle sighed. Of course, they were on show! Not that the driver could hear through the glass. She glanced out the window, then, driven by a devilish impulse, she moved closer to him, snuggling against his chest.

He stiffened. "What are you doing?"

"Trying to look realistically newly married." She pointed out the window. "For them."

Rico swore as a motorcycle came abreast, the pillion rider brandishing a camera. "Give us a kiss," the cameraman yelled.

Rico grabbed his cell phone and rapped out a sharp order to some unfortunate on the other end. Instantly a car moved up and edged the bike away.

"I was just about to oblige them," Danielle said impishly.

Rico threw her a black look, his brows meeting in a dark line.

"Oh, we're here," she said with relief as the car swept through the impressive arched entrance to the San Lorenzo Hotel.

As hard as he tried to pretend that Danielle wasn't having any effect on his equilibrium, Rico knew he lied. And he never lied. Especially not to himself.

So he forced himself to face up to the fact that Danielle Sinclair was crawling under his skin. That he'd wanted to kiss her properly, his mouth hot and hard on hers, in the church today. That the brief brush of his lips against hers had been totally unsatisfactory. That he liked having her tucked beneath his arm as they'd circulated earlier. Now he watched broodingly as she moved from table to table, speaking to couples, a warm smile for an elderly woman, a hug for a friend in a wheelchair.

The cake had been cut and the bouquet thrown. It was time for them to leave.

Time to put his plan into action.

Over the past few days, every time he'd met Danielle's clear grey-green eyes, a curious reluctance about what he intended to do had shifted inside him. But then he steeled himself, his lips firming into a brutally hard line.

*Lucia.* He waited for the familiar stab of emptiness to fill him—the numb loneliness had become oddly comforting and held none of the turbulent confusion that Danielle aroused.

But the darkness eluded him as he searched in vain for Lucia's wraithlike memory. Hell, if Lucia was not enough, the memory of his father's pale face in the critical care section of St. Joseph's hospital in Milan should be sufficient to stiffen his resolve. After he'd heard from his lawyer about Kim's surprising change of heart, he'd flown out from the Middle East and the latest kidnap crisis he'd been involved in barely making it to his father's side in time after an unexpected stroke. All he had to do now was fulfil his father's wishes. Wishes that dovetailed very nicely—

A heavy hand clapped his shoulder. "Everything okay?" Ken Pascal asked.

Rico shook himself free of his demons and nodded, and Pascal moved away. Like his own gaze, the Sinco security chief's eyes swept the room out of force of habit—despite the presence of the army of plainclothes security in the room.

Nothing would happen to Danielle.

Almost against his will, Rico sought her out.

She stood, slender and poised. A fitted sheath in the not-quite-white-but-ivory that modern brides favoured fell in soft, silky folds to her feet. His mouth flattened. The convention was a lie. After all, what woman today could truthfully wear a white gown? Instead they pretended, insisting that ivory wasn't white. It was a lie. A ridiculous lie. Besides, no man expected a virgin bride in today's society.

He didn't need an innocent. He wanted a woman who knew the score; a woman he could walk away from when it was done.

A woman like Danielle Sinclair, who despite her coolness, was a thoroughly modern female. Her silky dress clung lovingly to her slim, supple body. Her long hair hung loose, with little wispy bits hanging onto her face looking sexily rumpled. A far cry from the efficient, ice-princess image she brandished the rest of the time.

His bride.

No! Rico's hands fisted at his sides. She would never be his bride. His bride was dead. Buried. Abruptly he turned away, shoving white-knuckled fists in his pockets.

"You must be pleased with yourself. It all went smoothly."

He swung around at the barely veiled animosity in Robert Sinclair's voice. Sinclair was gazing at his daughter, a peculiar expression on his face. "She looks beautiful—so like her mother."

Rico wished Sinclair would shut up. He didn't need him repeating what he'd noticed all by himself: that Danielle glowed. Nor did he need any reminder of Rose Sinclair. What could he say to the man? *I'm sorry Rose Sinclair died because some damned worthless drunk ploughed into her car? Sorry for the hell Danielle endured being trapped with her mother's dead body?* And what about the most painful apology of all: *Sorry that Rose changed seats with me. It should've been me who died that day, not the mother of two teenage daughters.*

Blindly he watched Danielle glide up to yet another couple. The man moved away, leaving her talking to a redhead.

Kimberly, Rico realised, with sudden intensity. He'd shadowed Danielle's every movement for a week and this was the first time the two sisters had been together since Kimberly's return on Friday.

"D'Alessio—"

"Better call me Rico, hmm? Seeing that we're family now." Rico shot Sinclair a mocking glance, then decided it wouldn't do to get into a fistfight with his supposed father-in-law before the reception had even ended and added placatingly, "I remember her as a teenager. She was always a considerate girl."

"As I said, she's like her mother." Sinclair's voice was gruff. "Watch her like a hawk, I don't want—" he stopped "—anything to happen to her."

Sinclair had to be remembering his wife's death. He didn't need to empathise with the bastard, to see his human side. Catching sight of his bride, Rico made his way across the room, his path unwavering. Far easier to view Sinclair as a cold, tyrannical tycoon than as a man who'd lost the woman he loved.

Anything but that.

Danielle watched Rico determinedly forging his way towards her, wearing that distant expression she hated. David detained him, and she sighed in relief.

"Are you sure that this wedding plan will work?" Kim's eyes held concern…and curiosity.

Suddenly Danielle wished she'd kept Kim in the dark about the reason for her impulsive "marriage". "Ken, Daddy and Rico are convinced. You try arguing with those three."

"An unholy trinity, for sure." Kim's laughter grated on Danielle's already frazzled nerves. "But this is more my kind of stunt than yours—marrying Daddy's newest board member to thwart some weirdo. You should've had my wedding to Bradley."

It would've been *her* wedding if her mother had lived, Danielle thought. A marriage between Bradley, Rose Sinclair's best friend's eldest son, and Danielle, had been her mother's fondest wish. But it hadn't been fated. Bradley had married Kim—as her sister had wanted. Her sister was happy. At last.

But she couldn't resist saying, "Tired of Bradley already?" while she watched Rico say something to David, clap him on the back and continue toward her.

"Gosh, no! That was a joke." Kim looked horrified that Danielle might have taken her seriously.

For once Danielle had had enough of her sister's peculiar sense of humour. Turning to Kim, she said, "Well, don't offer him around if you mean to keep him."

"Dani—" Danielle winced at the old childhood name "—you didn't really want Bradley did you? That was all Mum's idea, wasn't it?" Insecurity clung to Kim's pretty features, and Danielle cursed herself for unsettling her sister.

"I was too young to know any better when our mothers paired us up. I was what…sixteen?…when they pronounced us a perfect match—and Bradley was only two years older. What did we know about life, love or relationships?"

The next year her mother had been killed and her life had changed forever. She'd withdrawn and struggled to come to terms with the trauma of the car accident and the loss of her mother. Almost twenty, Bradley had wanted to party, have fun, not provide emotional support for a fragile girl whose world had collapsed.

At seventeen she'd careened from Bradley's boy-next-door friendship to a year of wild infatuation. Her eyes rested on the object of that illicit infatuation as Carly Campbell waylaid him.

"So you don't mind that I…dated…Bradley, that we're married?"

Kim had chased Bradley with the tenacity of a seasoned hunter after the trophy of a lifetime. The man hadn't stood a chance. "Not at all. We never loved each other."

"Never?" Kim sounded strange.

Danielle shook her head. "Never," she repeated. Rico had shaken off Carly Campbell and was heading toward them.

Kim gave a theatrical shudder. "Rico D'Alessio scares me to death."

Given the opening she wanted, Danielle asked softly, "Why did you do it, Kim?"

Her sister's skin paled to a waxy shade whiter than the petals of the flowers on the tables. "I had to. It was making me unhappy so I told Bradley—and he said I had to confess to the authorities. He said he'd come with me. Bradley refused to marry me until I'd cleared Rico's name."

Horror swept over Danielle. If it hadn't been for Bradley…Rico would've remained under a cloud. Bradley had made Kim face the consequences of her actions. But he'd stood by her. Momentarily Danielle felt envious. He must love her sister, flaws and all.

"Why did you accuse Rico in the first place?" Suddenly she wanted to shake Kim.

Kim's eyes brimmed with transparent tears. "Oh, Danielle. Don't you remember what it was like? No, I don't suppose you do. You were so calm after Mom died. And I was confused!" Kim's voice started to wobble.

"Hush." Danielle bit back her irritated response and put a gentle hand on her sister's arm. "Don't work yourself up." Had no one noticed *her* pain, *her* anguish?

"Sorry." Kim gave a tremulous smile. "You said you knew nothing about life when you were sixteen. Well, nor did I. I was fifteen—"

"—almost sixteen."

"My mind was a muddle." But she didn't meet Danielle's eyes.

Danielle frowned, wanting to dig deeper. But she didn't need a scene, or reports of an altercation between her and Kim. Her questions would have to wait.

Rico had almost reached them. He looked determined, his jaw hard. Danielle didn't want him confronting Kim. Her sister must've had the same thought, because she muttered something incomprehensible, brushed a quick kiss across Danielle's cheek and disappeared into the throng.

As Rico closed the door of the bridal suite behind him, Danielle started.

Rico pushed himself away from the door, his gaze narrowing to dark slits, and took a step into the sitting area. She stared at him wide-eyed, desperately casting around for something light and humorous to say to dissolve the rapidly escalating tension as he advanced into the room.

The ornate suite was decorated in shades of cream and gold. Long-stemmed lilies stood in two tall vases on a low table in front of the couch where she waited. But the details meant nothing to Danielle as she focused breathlessly on Rico.

He stopped inches from her, shrugged off his jacket and hurled it onto the adjacent chair with barely leashed force.

"You were right to fear me, to think I want more." He flung the words into the silence of the room, shattering the uneasy truce they'd established.

Panic fluttered through her. This was Rico, she told herself. He wouldn't harm her. If he'd wanted to, he could've hurt her anytime in the past two weeks.

She tipped her head back. "So what *do* you want?" she challenged.

He ripped his bow tie loose and threw it after the jacket. She slid her tongue over suddenly dry lips and lifted her bare feet to tuck them beneath her. The soft satin of her bridal gown caressed her legs, increasing her awareness of tingling skin. Mesmerised, Danielle watched his hand return to his throat and undo the top button. Hastily she flicked her gaze upward, away from the triangle of exposed tanned flesh, and met his knowing gaze.

"What do you think I want?" he asked throatily.

Her heart leaped. She forced herself to breathe slowly, to control her reaction to him. "Not *that!* You could've had that years ago!"

"You were little more than a child…then. But things have changed. I'm no longer a married man, for one."

The tight mouth, glittering eyes and set jaw didn't belong to a man about to succumb to passion. "No, that's not what you want. It's…something else," she said slowly.

"I want what I lost."

His words lay between them like a wall.

Danielle frowned. "But you've got a position on the Sinco board. And your shares have been reissued. I processed the paperwork, remember?" she said, referring to all the forms she'd filled in while he sat in her office.

"It's not enough."

"Daddy will talk to Bradley soon." She paused as he shook his head. "So what more do you want?" The words emerged breathlessly under his dark stare.

His voice barely above a whisper, he murmured, "I want a real marriage. Monday morning we go to a registry office and validate today's ceremony."

Rico wanted to marry her. For real. Danielle's chest tightened, and blood pounded in her head until each thud-thud throbbed. But why? She shook her head, trying to clear the confusion. What was he after? It certainly wasn't as if her body held any appeal. *"Why?"*

"Because I want a son, an heir."

Sick disappointment churned in her stomach. He didn't need a sham marriage to regain his reputation. "You mislead me. Deliberately. Do you know how much that *really* pains me—what you did was tantamount to lying!"

"Pain?" He spoke so softly she strained to hear him. "I know about real pain. The kind that rips into you like a knife, and hacks your heart out until there is nothing left but a numb, black hole. No life. No feeling. Nothing." He stared past her, his eyes unfocused. "After Kim's trumped up statement I had no choice, I had to leave the country. Your father made sure of that."

"How—" Danielle broke off too scared to ask. What had her father done?

"Your father convinced my wife that I would go to prison if I was charged—whether I'd done anything to Kim or not— unless I turned over my shares and left the country. Lucia was frantic with worry. I had no choice. We left." He shut his eyes and the cords in his neck stood out. "A month later Lucia lost our baby. Less than a week afterwards she killed herself."

Danielle shuddered at the rawness in his voice. She tried to block out the agony etched on his face. "You can't hold that against my father—"

"Oh, yes, I can." His eyes flicked open, boring into her, bleak and merciless. "He convinced Lucia that I would go to prison. Even more than she hated the idea of being married to an adulterous bastard who preyed on impressionable young girls, Lucia couldn't bear the idea of her child's father being a convict. It killed her."

*Oh, God.* Danielle pressed a balled fist against her mouth, the knuckles ridging her lips.

"Lucia begged me to leave New Zealand, to flee like a coward—even though I wanted to stand trial, show the world that I'd been set up. Your father stripped me of everything that I had. My dignity. My reputation. My wife and my child."

The silence stretched, but she could think of nothing to say that wouldn't sound awfully banal and patronising. At last she said, "I *can't* give you a real marriage."

"Because you're a Sinclair?" His hand went to his chest, and the second shirt button popped open. "A princess? And I'm a *paesano?*"

Riveted, she stared at the hand that was now undoing button number three. *"Paesano?"* She frowned at the unfamiliar word.

"It means peasant, Princess." He yanked the shirt over his head.

Her breath caught at the sight of the solid strength of his arms and shoulders, of his bronzed chest, with the beautifully defined muscle. "No! I don't want to marry anyone, because—"

He interrupted with an ugly laugh. "You're off the hook, Princess. I only want a temporary wife." He threw the shirt away from him with unnecessary force.

Temporary wife. She averted her eyes from his bare chest and looked him straight in the eye, hoping he wouldn't notice her flaming cheeks. "So why do you want a temporary wife at all?"

He was so close that she could see the dark line shadowing his jaw, smell the scent of his skin mixed with aftershave— the unique scent that was Rico. She held her breath, determined to shut out the impact he had on her senses.

She froze as he placed his hands on the couch back, trapping her between his arms, and lowered his face to hers. "You're going to give me a son, in exchange for the child I lost."

*Oh, God!*

The pain was as sharp as hot ice splintering inside her chest. It ripped her apart and she stifled an exclamation. Ducking under his arm, she skittered away to the opposite corner of the couch. He let her go. Running an unsteady hand through her fine hair, she said with more conviction than she felt, "I can't do this, Rico. I can't marry you."

"Oh, yes, you can. And you'll give me a child. Mine. I want him to be born legitimate, to carry the D'Alessio name."

# Five

*Mine.*

His child! "That's why you suggested today's charade?" Danielle challenged him, outraged and shocked by the lengths he'd gone to. "So that you could get revenge?"

His eyes flickered.

Bingo! "You wanted to trap me into giving you a child." Danielle flung the words at him, rising to her feet and almost bursting into wild laughter. But she had a nasty suspicion that once she started, she wouldn't be able to stop hysteria from taking over. "It had nothing to do with protecting me, saving me from some monster. Or even regaining your lost reputation. Gosh, but you did a grand sales job. I believed you!" That hurt. She'd secretly hoped his help meant that he had a soft spot for her. Stupid!

Another thought struck. "Does this man even exist? Or is he a figment of your imagination, a phantom that you've got us all chasing?" she demanded. "Strange, I'd never thought of you as cruel."

He caught her wrist, his eyes empty, and put her back down onto the couch. "Stalking is not my style. He's no phantom. Never underestimate him."

*Never underestimate Rico.* Intimidating, dangerous, yet he didn't scare her. She didn't even bother to fight free of his grasp. "And the wedding? Was that part of the original plan?"

He shrugged, and a wave of silky hair fell forward onto his brow. "Okay. I admit it, the wedding was convenient. A means to an end."

She resisted the urge to push the errant lock back with her free hand. Strange that his hair looked so soft, when the man himself was so hard. Ruthlessly suppressing the effect that a single lock and all that bare skin had on her, Danielle focused on a growing realisation. This wasn't some spur-of-the-moment idea. He'd thought it all out, then jumped at the opportunity when it came his way. "How long have you been planning this?" she asked suddenly.

His mouth twisted. "Since the call came from my lawyer that Kim had recanted. But my original plan had to be abandoned."

So he *had* planned it! She recoiled, and his fingers tightened around her wrist. She shouldn't be surprised. Being hell-bent on revenge would've made up for some of the humiliation he'd suffered.

"Oh?" she invited.

"Kim decided to get married, and bigamy is a little too… difficult."

He'd planned to go after Kim! Danielle shut her eyes at the thought of Rico married to Kim…he would've knocked the life out of her flighty, neurotic sister. At least Kim was safe in Bradley's care. As for herself…

When she opened her eyes, she'd made her decision. "There's no way I can do what you want," she said flatly, flexing her hands in his grasp, trying not to let his touch warm her. It was the absolute truth, for more reasons than he knew.

She'd finally escaped her father's control, she wasn't submitting to another man's demands. Especially a man who required only a convenient womb.

"If that's your final answer, I'll have to go to plan B."

He let go of her hand. She rubbed the sensitised skin at her wrist and felt a chilling sense of loss at the broken connection. "Plan B?"

"You didn't think I wouldn't have a fallback plan did you, Princess?" His tone was gentle, but his eyes scorched across the small space that separated them.

With mounting unease, she asked. "What is plan B?"

He placed a knee on the edge of the couch, and the move brought him closer to her. "Why, marry Kimberly, of course."

"But she's already married. And you're married to me."

"A pretend marriage or have you forgotten?" The look he gave her was pointed.

It hurt to have him to remind her.

Slowly with the infinite patience she'd always used to convince Kim that some madcap plan would not work, she said, "You can't marry Kim. You've already abandoned that plan."

"Maybe not. Marrying you would certainly be easier…in the eyes of most of the world we're married already." He smiled, a cold smile that bared his teeth but failed to melt the ice in his eyes.

A chill of foreboding crept down her arms. She rocked back into the corner of the couch and hugged her knees to her chest.

When he shrugged carelessly, more tension wound through

her, not helped by the words that followed. "But seeing that you won't oblige—I have no choice but to seek out Kim."

"What are you going to do to Kim?" Danielle's fingernails bit into her palms under the folds of her dress.

"Put an end to her marriage."

*Over her dead body!* Not after all the years that she'd spent watchdogging her sister, not when she'd finally seen Kim safely married.

"I spent the past four years making enough money to last me a lifetime. And on my wife's death I inherited a fortune I never wanted. I never touched a cent of Lucia's money while she was alive, I wanted us to make our own way—without her family's help." Eyes blacker than night cut into her, no hint of softness in the bottomless pits. "But now she's gone and I'll use every cent of her legacy to break Kimberly's marriage to Lester."

Armed with a fortune to burn and his explosive need for revenge…he'd be lethal.

"Believe me, Kim won't withstand the methods I intend to use. She's already eaten by guilt." He paused a moment, cocking his head. "How long do you think she'll hold out? I give her six months at the most."

Damn him. He was too hard, too ruthless. His drive for revenge at all costs wouldn't only destroy her sister's marriage, it would destroy Kim, too. She *had* to dissuade him. "How can you even contemplate going through with this?"

"She destroyed my marriage, my life, without a qualm. I was driven out of your father's business, out of the country on a lie. I couldn't stop my wife from miscarrying. I couldn't save her from the dark demons that your father unleashed—she *died!* You tell me why I should hesitate for a second."

His eyes flashed with anger…and something else…despair, she realised, feeling sicker by the minute. "What if you burn in hell, doesn't that scare you?"

"Hell?" He laughed, a harsh sound with absolutely no humour. "I'm already there."

She stared into his implacable eyes and knew he was past reason, driven by a depth of rage that exceeded anything she'd ever experienced. So she decided to switch tactics. "What happens once the child is born?" Danielle knew it was fool-hardy to involve herself in the fate of his unborn child.

"A divorce. An agreement with the mother forsaking all rights to the child."

*Oh, Kim!* She couldn't let that happen to Kim. Briefly she considered confiding in Bradley. Not only was Rico after his position on the Sinco board, he wanted Kim, too. Bradley loved Kim; he'd be outraged. It would all end in tragedy. A tragedy her family had initiated.

Rico wanted a child to mend the wrongs done to him in the past—and given his hard resolve, Danielle doubted he'd abandon his mission. Yet despite his bitterness, Danielle had no difficulty picturing Rico as a father; he'd be kind, caring, and he'd love the baby with all his heart.

Pity wrenched her heart at the choice he'd already made. The baby would have no mother. How could he commit a child to such a life?

"But, of course, all that could be circumvented if you marry me legally. Tomorrow." He interrupted her thoughts and bent closer.

Instantly her traitorous body responded to his softer-than-silk voice. Deceptively soft, Danielle thought bitterly. His breath brushed across her lips and goose bumps flooded her skin. She shuddered, resenting the thrall he held her in. Damn, damn him. He'd manipulated them all. Her father, David, Ken…and herself.

And damn her wretched body for wanting him.

She paused, tipping her head sideways. But…if she really

did marry him, let him make love to her…then… Her heart jerked. The solution struck her. So simple. She could still out-manoeuvre him. Dare she do it?

The opportunity to discover what it was like to make love to a man, and not just any man, a man she'd hungered for years ago, had been handed to her on a plate. Rico wanted a temporary wife. If she waited all her life, she might never get another chance. Because happily-ever-after was one expectation she couldn't fulfil.

So why was she hesitating?

*She* was the innocent party in all this. *She* need feel no compunction about using him. With one stroke she could save Kim's marriage and gain herself pleasure for as long as it lasted. Because there was one thing she didn't doubt: Rico D'Alessio would be dynamite between the sheets.

But she wasn't going to let him think her a pushover. Her jaw tilting, she released her knees, setting her feet firmly on the ground. "What if I can't bear for you to touch me?"

It sounded so ridiculous. She lifted her chin another notch.

"I don't think that will be a problem, Princess," he purred.

She wanted to hit him for his confidence. "You going to force me?" she charged rashly.

His eyes froze. "Force won't be necessary. Despite the initial accusations, rape never was to my taste."

A hand reached out. She felt his fingertip against the side of her uptilted cheek. Slowly it moved down, following a thin, burning line like a brand, until it stopped at the corner of her mouth, then moved inward to rest on the bow of her lips.

"These lips will respond when I kiss them—you know that as well as I do. So let's drop the pretence, hmm?" He lowered his big body, settling himself beside her, his thigh touching hers.

Heat exploded within her. "What are you doing?" Her voice rose. The last thing she needed was Rico finding out how much—

"I thought I'd prove that you won't find me repulsive, and replace my fingertip with my mouth," he murmured, and all coherent thought fled.

Her heart thundered. Panicked, she put her palms against his bare chest and shoved. "Don't worry, I don't need that kind of persuasion. I'll marry you."

Her words had the effect she told herself she wanted: his hand lifted and he moved away to the other end of the couch, giving her space. "You'll give me the son I want?"

She hesitated, then gave an abrupt nod. "On one condition. That tomorrow you sign an agreement promising never to go after Kim. That you'll leave her alone."

"It would never hold up in court."

She blinked. His dark gaze held determination and passion. "I know. But strangely enough I trust you to honour it."

Some of the chill left his eyes. "Okay, I'll live with that."

Danielle shivered. She doubted he'd still consider it binding if he ever discovered her deception, but that was a risk she'd have to take.

Standing in the hustle and bustle of Queen Street outside the registry office on Monday morning, Danielle knew in her heart of hearts she'd always consider Saturday's ceremony as her wedding day—not today's grey proceeding with the dull-voiced public official whose monotone did little to block out the enormity of Rico's latest deceit.

"Okay, Mrs. D'Alessio, how about lunch to celebrate?" Rico suggested. He'd been cautious ever since she'd learned it took three days to obtain a marriage licence—a licence he'd managed to produce from his pocket forty minutes ago.

He'd been so certain of her that he'd applied for a licence nearly a week ago.

That maddened her.

"I must get back to work," she said in a stiff little voice. "I've already been out for over two hours."

In addition to getting married, there'd been a visit to Steele & Hancock where she and Rico had signed the prenuptial contract she'd hastily arranged this morning, the terms of which had almost caused Darien Steele's eyebrows to hit the ceiling. At the last moment Rico had tried to insert a settlement into the contract.

Guilt money, she'd thought, even as Darien Steele tried to talk her into accepting it. Of course she'd refused Rico's offer. He'd have to live with his conscience. For her part she wanted to keep the terms of the exchange clear—for revenge he got a child. As far as Rico was concerned, she got nothing except his promise to leave Kim alone, and a watertight clause to vacate her house on demand. Nothing to muddy the waters later.

"Surely getting married deserves some celebration?" Rico's slow smile made her pulse quicken against her will. "I took the liberty of telling Cynthia that I was taking my new bride to lunch, seeing that we've delayed the honeymoon until you're less busy.

"I've booked a table," he cajoled. "You deserve some time out."

Rico was right. She *was* feeling stressed and out of sorts. Perhaps they could call a truce, starting with lunch. After all, they were going to be living together and trying to...

Her breath quickened as erotic images of what might happen later filled her mind. Her voice husky, she said, "You're right. Lunch would be good."

Danielle expected him to take her to Sergio's—a very ex-

clusive Italian restaurant—or perhaps to one of the finer
French establishments. Instead she was pleasantly surprised
when he led her to a shopfront dominated by Japanese influ-
ence in a quiet side street. Inside the décor was stark but
serene; modern black lacquer and white rice-paper screens,
with splashes of colour provided by scarlet pots filled with
leafy bamboo. They sat on low pallets and the exquisite
morsels of food arrived on flat white platters—works of art
that made her mouth water.

How decadent to be out to lunch in this exotic restaurant
with its interlocking screens that blocked out other diners.
*Like an assignation.* That thought, and the decidedly sensual
food, made Danielle's stomach churn with excitement.

"Try this." Rico held out a piece of sushi.

Delicately Danielle took it from his hand, careful not to let
her lips brush his fingers. Taste sensations exploded on her
tongue; she closed her eyes and moaned in delight. When she
opened them he was staring at her with a strange expression.

"What's the matter?"

"It's good to be with a woman who loves food. Somehow
I never associated such an appetite for food with you."

Instantly Danielle felt self-conscious. "I'm making a pig of
myself," she said ruefully, eyeing the empty platter in front of
her.

"No! Never apologise for eating with passion and enjoy-
ment. I simply thought you'd be too—" he hesitated "—restrained."

What word had come to his mind first? Did he think her
colourless? Or had he heard the cruel rumours that dubbed her
frigid, an Ice Queen?

She looked away, blinking rapidly as her throat tightened.

"You remind me of my youngest sister, she eats like that,
too."

Quickly she glanced back at him. Rico hadn't been mocking her. And he'd never before spoken about his family to her. He'd always been contained, remote.

Her father's perfect protégé.

She leaned forward. "You have sisters? How many? Tell me about them."

"Two. Claudia is twenty-seven—three years younger than me—and married to an Australian. She's pregnant—she already has one daughter—and lives in Melbourne." His smile was soft. "Bella is the baby of the family. She's twenty-two and stays in Milan with my parents. My mother despairs of ever marrying her off."

How must they have felt when Rico had been questioned by the police? His younger sister was the same age as she was. Four years ago Bella would've been eighteen. Had they believed him guilty? Kim's actions must have affected them all.

Danielle stared at the platter, suddenly no longer hungry. Would she ever be able to come to terms with what had been done to Rico? And, more important, would she ever be able to forgive him for choosing her as the scapegoat for her family's actions?

She feared not.

By the time they returned to the office, Cynthia had already left and a pile of messages awaited Danielle's attention. She sighed, knowing that they would not be leaving early today.

Through Cynthia's office she caught a glimpse of Rico's dark, tough profile and ducked her head before he caught her staring, and tried to block out the tap-tap of his fingers on the keyboard. A pile of questionnaires were stacked beside her. Several staff members had recently undergone extensive psychometric testing. She needed to analyse the results and update their personnel files before she called them in to discuss the outcomes and help them map out career paths.

Rico—her husband, she amended, refusing to look in his direction—was a distraction she didn't need. For the next half hour, uninterrupted by anything except the occasional rustle of paper and the clatter of keyboards, Danielle struggled to process the pile of forms in front of her. Without Cynthia in the outer office, the silence simmered.

Eventually Danielle rolled the chair back and stood, stretching her arms to ease the tightness that lurked in her shoulders—a symptom of a much deeper tension. She strolled through Cynthia's office and tried not to notice that Rico's hands had stilled on the keyboard.

"Where are you going?"

She rolled her eyes to the ceiling, safe in the knowledge that her back was firmly turned, and answered, "Down the passage."

"Exactly where down the passage?" he asked with exaggerated patience.

"To the little pink room."

His voice was closer than she'd expected. "I'll walk you there."

She hadn't heard him move. Her neck prickling, she swivelled and found him right behind her. "This is ridiculous, Rico."

He confronted her. "No, it's not. It's a sensible precaution. It's late and the building is empty."

"Fine. Please yourself," she huffed, then turned on her heel and strode away, conscious of him following her down the deserted corridor. The offices on either side were empty of their occupants, and the large open-plan office space near the cloakrooms looked desolate, like a railway station abandoned after the commuter rush.

When she opened the cloakroom door Rico's hand closed around her elbow.

"Let me take a look around first," he commanded, releasing her. Only when he was satisfied that no one skulked in any of the cubicles did he come out.

"I thought you said it was pink," he murmured.

"You know what I meant." Danielle stepped past him.

As she closed the outer door, he hooked his foot around it and murmured, "This door stays open."

A burst of exasperated air escaped her. He waved four fingers at her. "Off you go, I'll be waiting."

Danielle stormed into the end cubicle, as far as she could get away from him, and banged the door shut. His soft laughter followed her, disrupting her peace even here.

Insolent, insufferable man!

When Danielle came out of the ladies' cloakroom, Rico studied her uptight expression with some amusement. "I'll escort you back to your office," he said with gentle irony.

She shot past him, indignation coming off her in waves. As he strode down the corridor behind her he couldn't help noticing, in true Italian fashion, how lovingly the ivory designer suit clung to her body, outlining her pert bottom, drawing his eyes to the angry sway of her hips, giving him ample opportunity to admire her long, slim legs striding out. He itched to reach out and stroke her bottom. Rico's lips curved. Perhaps not a good idea given her current level of irritation with him.

Instead he shoved his hands deep into his pockets and, averting his gaze, he studied her narrow shoes as he strolled behind her. The dainty black heels contrasted with the caramel colour of the rest of the shoe which matched her bare skin perfectly—making them appear endless. Her legs were taut and sleek, the colour of Manuka honey—

Ah. *Hell.* Frustrated, he shook his head. Not even her feet could distract him from the understated sensuality she exuded.

"Are you following me?" The elegantly shod feet had stopped. She swung round, her usually serene eyes smouldering, hungry for a fight, and so close that he could see the smoky silver clouding the irises.

"I'm supposed to keep an eye on you, remember?" he said, fighting to control the heat surging though his lower gut as their eyes warred. He was overreacting. This…this madness resulted from too many years of forced abstinence, because Danielle Sinclair was not the kind of woman who would normally attract him.

Icy, cool-eyed almost-blondes left him cold.

Except, she didn't look cool right now. Her eyes glowed with silver heat, and the streaks in her hair shone like ancient amber. She looked fiery and alive. Suddenly Rico had a mad, consuming desire to throw caution to the winds and take her in his arms.

"You're invading my space," she said, in that private-school, touch-me-not voice.

She provoked him. Hell, she made him burn.

He struggled to keep his tone humorous. "Trust me, I'm keeping well out of your personal space."

Her delicately arched brows shot up. "*This* is keeping out of my space?" Deliberately she gazed measuringly at the space that separated them.

She had a point. From this close he could appreciate the silky texture of her skin, count each long, dark lash that circled her eyes. But instead of admitting it and backing off, some primal impulse made him respond to the cool challenge in her gaze by moving closer until their hips touched.

He watched her pupils dilate and her eyes turn stormy.

"Princess, *now* I'd say I'm in your space," he taunted.

"D'Alessio," her voice held a warning note, "you're in my face."

A rush of reckless energy filled him. "In your face? Not yet, Princess. But that can change."

Without waiting for an answer, he swiftly bent his head and kissed her.

Rico tasted her gasp. Immediately he took advantage of her parted lips, swirled his tongue past their lush softness and sank into her mouth. Adrenaline shafted through him. He dropped his hands to the edge of the desk behind her, and gripped the wood tightly, his hips sinking closer, his thigh shifting between hers.

He withdrew and teasingly nibbled her bottom lip. She moaned. Her hands clutched at his shoulders, and the restless friction of her fingers against the fine cotton of his shirt drove him wild. He licked the corner of her mouth until her tongue came out to brush his, then retreated. With a groan he followed it. He didn't stop to think; he simply unleashed his senses and let his mouth go wild, bending her back until with a gasp she stretched out on the desk. Immediately Rico followed her down, his thigh still between hers. Propping his weight on his elbows, careful not to trap her under his bulk, he slanted his mouth across hers and demanded a response.

She didn't let him down. *Dio,* but the woman could kiss! She kissed with a reckless abandon he'd never associated with the calm façade she presented to the world.

He couldn't stop the groan that burst from him and, totally enthralled, he closed his eyes and lost himself in the vortex of heat and turbulence, biting at her mouth with a desperation that was frighteningly foreign. His head started to spin. Forcing himself to slow down, he slid his lips over the soft skin beside the engaging dimple, trailed a row of frantic kisses down her chin, down…his mouth open against her smooth, silky neck.

Jackknifing away from her, he unfastened the buttons of her ivory jacket with clumsy fingers and, pushing the edges apart, stared at the curves of her breasts beneath the clinging vanilla silk camisole. His breath caught.

Mother of God but she was beautiful. All pale-golden skin and slender bones, framed by the delicate lace that edged the camisole.

So soft, so feminine.

His hand lay reverently against her—it looked dark and too masculine against her paleness. Damn, but it had been a long time since he'd touched a woman's skin.

Tension prickled at the thought, but he thrust the underlying anxiety away, focusing on the woman stretched beneath him. He brushed his fingers over the fine fabric, imagining the texture of the flesh beneath and noticed that his hand shook.

*Hell!*

Shoving the camisole aside, he hurriedly dealt with the front snap of her bra and gazed hungrily at the magnificent curves with the dark-pink hardening tips. Need swept through him, making him aware of the ache between his thighs. Soon! Bending, he closed his mouth over the provocative nipple. She gasped and her body arched against his. A groan shuddered deep inside him. Gently he pursed his lips on the peak of flesh, tasting her like a starved man faced with a banquet.

He slid a hand down between their bodies, under her hindering skirt, until his fingers found the valley between her thighs. Whimpers burst from her mouth. Releasing the berry-like nipple he surged upward to cover her mouth roughly with his, feeling his control strip as she bowed against his fingers and more keening sounds of pleasure broke from her throat and vibrated against his lips.

Impatiently Rico yanked at her skirt, wanting to touch her right *there*…where she was hottest, needing to feel her moist response to him.

She wriggled, and the skirt gave. He arched back, twisting to free her from his weight, and, unable to resist, glanced down.

The glimpse of white lace covering the intimate mound between her thighs was like a blast of cold water. Memories, as fresh as her floral scent, of a similar pair of pristine panties fashioned from flowered lace spun inside his head creating a turmoil that thundered in his ears.

*Dio!* What in heaven's name was he doing?

He straightened, raked an unsteady hand through the inky hair that had fallen onto his face, reluctant to confront the dazed desire in her lake-grey eyes.

"Why are you stopping?" Her voice sounded husky. "I thought you meant…"

Incapable of responding, he sucked in deep lungfuls of air.

"Haven't you got protection?" she asked.

A fragment of sound, somewhere between laughter and pain, escaped him. Why would he have protection? He hadn't wanted a woman in years. A shudder shook his taut frame as he gazed at the woman draped over the desk, her pale-golden skin standing out against the sheen of the rich cherry wood beneath her.

When he finally lifted his gaze to meet her clear eyes, the vulnerability he encountered caused some aching emotion to clog his throat. He swallowed convulsively. Her eyes weren't the colour of dark-purple velvet, nor did her hair tumble in ebony curls over voluptuous curves.

Instantly his stomach cramped with self-loathing. He hadn't expected such raw passion, hotter and more impulsive than anything he'd ever experienced. Nor had he expected the shame that had followed. Up until now he'd been in command, but the balance of power had shifted. Suddenly he'd lost it, and *she* was in control, a sensual stranger who knew exactly what she wanted…no sign of the cool woman he'd worked beside. And he wasn't sure if he could handle the change.

Could he go through with his planned revenge? For the first time doubt assailed him.

She wasn't Lucia. Pain and panic seized him. Suddenly it was no longer a simple matter of procreation or revenge. *Dio!* He *had* to face the knowledge that he'd betrayed his dead wife's memory. *Damn.* He had to be desperate.

The last thing he'd ever expected had happened: Danielle Sinclair had turned him on.

# Six

"Rico?" Danielle prodded.

Pushing away from the hard desk against her back, she reached up and tangled her arms around his neck. For an instant he resisted her gentle tugs, and she thought all was lost. Then he sighed softly and his head came closer, causing her pulse to quicken. At the last moment he ducked his face into the curve of her shoulder, instead of kissing her as she'd intended.

"Of course, we don't need protection, do we?" she whispered softly, trying for a hint of seduction. Heck, what did she know about seduction? But, darn it, she'd try her best. "The whole point of all this…is a child, isn't it?"

A pang of guilt at her deceit pierced her as his large body trembled. Ignoring it, she lifted her head. From her vantage point, she couldn't see his eyes, only the half-moons of his eyelids, his thick, impossibly long lashes, and the skin pulled taut across his cheekbones. But she could sense his anguish. Was he suffering from misgivings? For a moment sympathy welled inside her. Then she tensed. His motives were far from pure. *He'd used her.*

If he backed off, he'd never make love to her, and she'd never know…

She couldn't let that happen.

Rico was her chance to catch up on the years she'd missed. In the confusing period after her mother's death, she'd been hamstrung with the responsibility of Kim and by her own innate discernment that hadn't let her bed the boys emboldened by a few beers at a student party and bent on a quick lay.

But Rico was different.

He was her husband! Pride, a peculiar kind of affection for him—despite his outrageous plan—and, of course, the ever-present sharp longing filled her. For heaven's sake, she *had* to get a grip. She couldn't afford to become addicted—or dependant—on Rico. She bit her lip. Their marriage wasn't intended to last. The seeds of its destruction were already sown. And if he discovered the truth…

The truth. Blindly she stared at the sexy dark stubble shadowing his jaw. When he found out, their temporary marriage would be finished. But at least she'd have memories to pull out one day, to cherish and treasure when all she had was a Sinco directorship to keep her warm at night.

Her hand hovered over his face, drawn by the need for contact. "Come on, we don't have a moment to waste." She touched his cheek, enjoying the masculine roughness under her fingertips.

His body went rigid, then he hauled himself up, away from her. Her hand dropped. And suddenly Danielle felt cold and very, very alone.

"Strange as it may seem, I can't do this." The back he presented to her was rigid. "Not yet."

Hurt seeped through her. Was she so undesirable? No, she refused to believe that. He'd been on fire for her. One minute he'd been tearing at her clothes, kissing her like a man in the grasp of a sexual thrall, the next moment he'd gone tense and silent.

"Are you saying you don't want to make l—" she caught herself "—have sex with me?"

He turned and his mouth twisted. She read the distaste in his eyes. "Do you really want to do it here? In your office? Spread-eagled on your desk?" He gestured at their surroundings. "Where we might be interrupted at any minute by cleaners?"

"We could lock the door," she suggested, fixing the familiar face-numbing smile in place, but the crude image he'd evoked of her sprawled across the desk made her flush, destroying the unique excitement and the sensuous yearning that had burgeoned inside her. He made it sound so…sordid.

Rico didn't smile back.

Slowly Danielle sat up and pulled her skirt down. In a desperate bid for equanimity she said, "It's no big deal. It's only a kiss." Even as she uttered them, she knew the words were a lie. It was far more than a kiss. But no way was she revealing that to Rico. Not while he stared at her as though she were a stranger.

Instead of the woman he'd married.

Married for real.

Today.

Rebuttoning her jacket with hands that trembled, she slid off the desk and almost said, "Hey, remember me? Danielle Sinclair? The woman you intend to impregnate?" But thought better of it. Rico didn't need to be reminded of who she was— she was still wearing the suit she'd worn in front of the celebrant, and the glittering eternity ring he'd slipped on her finger this morning rubbed against the antique ring he'd given her on Saturday.

But everything had changed. Under her jacket her nipples were tight and hard, her bra undone. As for Rico, under the veneer of contempt he looked shaken, his hair rumpled where he'd run his hands through the overlong strands.

"Rico." She placed a hand on his shoulder. "What's the matter?"

For a moment he didn't move. Then he dropped his head and gave a bitter laugh and his whole body shook. "Trust me, you wouldn't understand."

She drew a deep breath and said carefully, "Perhaps you should trust me…tell me what's bothering you."

Silence.

Then his hands dropped to his sides. "I can't trust you."

Flinching, she slid her hand off his shoulder and stepped away. She wasn't really surprised at his bleak words, although she hadn't expected the raw pain that seared her. But in the end, he was right not to trust her. But not for the obvious reason. "Because I'm a Sinclair?"

He ignored her challenge. "If I trusted you—" he paused "—it would be a betrayal."

She stared at his hands clenched against his thighs, fighting to fathom out what he was thinking. "Why?"

"Hell, it's myself I can't trust." He lifted his head. His eyes were a molten mix of turbulent emotions. Danielle recognised anger, wariness and something hot and dangerous. "What in hell's name am I thinking of? To consider sleeping with a Sinclair?"

His words hit like a rain of blows, and a second burst of pain exploded inside her. But she refused to react with the anger she suspected he was trying to goad her into. Instead she asked, "Are you saying that you want to try this some other way?"

"Other way?"

"There are medical procedures, you know. You don't actually need to *touch* me." Why was she suggesting this? She *wanted* him to make love to her, *needed* to know how it felt to be a real woman. The medical route would screw it all up.

For an instant he hesitated, and she waited tensely. Was he going to call the whole elaborate scheme off? Or was she so repugnant that he'd go for the sterile, medical option to avoid the necessity of touching her? And send her hopes up in smoke?

Seconds dragged past, then his eyes hardened, and the jumble of emotions disappeared behind his formidable control. "No! I want to be sure the child is mine. A D'Alessio. I want the world...particularly your sister and your father—" his eyes stabbed at her "—to know *exactly* how this conception took place."

A public revenge.

Nothing less would satisfy him. It hurt more than any pain she'd ever experienced. Even more than—

No! She dared not think about that now. Danielle glanced away, determined not to reveal any vulnerability to him. He had the power to bruise her soul if she let him.

But she was damned if she'd let him discover the power that he held over her. Pulling herself together, she decided he didn't deserve her...sympathy. Whatever happened, Rico had it coming.

Danielle didn't break the silence on the drive home. Bone tired, she concentrated on the road, checking and rechecking her rearview mirror, regularly slowing and changing lanes as Rico had instructed her. Rico had the passenger visor down, and out of the corner of her eye she watched him use the small mirror to monitor whether they were being followed. She turned off into a narrow street in Newmarket and after a sweeping glance of the street nosed the BMW into the drive of a tall, narrow double-storey townhouse. The hum of the electronic garage door filled the air after she killed the engine. A click signalled the door's closing and the humming stopped.

The sudden silence rang between them. She waited for Rico to speak. When he didn't, Danielle suppressed a sigh, and climbed out.

The garage accessed directly into a small lobby off the kitchen, Rico followed her into the house. She knew he'd been here earlier in the week to go over the place with a fine-toothed comb. Afterwards he'd ordered additional security measures before he'd pronounced himself satisfied. His clothes hung upstairs in the master bedroom. Parsons, her father's trusted butler, had personally overseen the transfer of her possessions and a suitcase of Rico's.

Parsons had fussed that the furnishings were too spare. Eventually she'd given in and picked a suite for the bedroom and living room from an upmarket furnishing catalogue to satisfy the butler. As Rico had insisted on a real marriage, she'd substituted her double bed with a vast king-size one. On the basis that it would at least give her and Rico acres of space between them.

It had been liberating making choices, taking decisions. Danielle had firmly suppressed the unexpected niggling of guilt, telling herself this was *her* house. Not Rico's. There was no need to consult him about choices she'd made. Because his stay was temporary. Yet, annoyingly, she'd found herself refraining from further catalogue shopping and resolving to go on a spree over the weekend.

Tiredly she hung up the car keys, dropped her briefcase and made for the freezer that she'd stocked on Friday, before the wedding—the pretend wedding. The one that had felt like the real thing. Spots danced in front of her eyes. Heck, she was tying herself up in knots. She no longer knew what was real and what was illusion.

She selected a frozen slab of lasagne, pulled off the cover and stuck it in the oven. Rico was checking the window catches, she could hear him moving around the sitting room, and a little later she heard his footsteps overhead. Hastily she set two places in the breakfast nook. Five minutes later he strolled into the kitchen. Danielle handed him a bottle of wine and a corkscrew.

"Need help, Princess?"

Relief shot through her at his casual tone. For once the taunting "Princess" didn't bother her. At least the dark cloud that had hung over him since *that* kiss had lifted—he was speaking to her again. "I'm perfectly able to open a bottle of wine. I simply thought you might want to do something useful."

"Ah."

Had he realised that all this security stuff was setting her teeth on edge? Not to mention the spiralling tension that his proximity evoked. A glass of wine would relax her and establish a pretence of congeniality between them. Last night they'd stayed in the suite at the San Lorenzo and today it had been business as usual. Tonight was the first time they'd been in a home together, like a normal married couple. Hardly surprising that she was a little edgy.

Rico handed her a glass, and she took a quick sip. The wine seeped through her, warming her. She offered him a smile. He returned it. Danielle started to relax.

It was going to be okay.

When the timer pinged, she took the lasagne out of the oven, scooped the contents onto two plates and set one before Rico.

"What is this?" he asked, frowning at his plate.

"Lasagne."

He poked it with a fork. "No." He shook his head emphatically. "Whatever that sorry dish is, I can assure you it's not lasagne. I'll cook you lasagne so you know the difference."

"*You'll* cook?" Danielle examined him across the countertop, looking for any oddity that might reveal he was an alien visiting from another planet. Her father had never as much as boiled an egg in all the years that she could remember.

"Of course."

There was no "of course" about it. She started to grin. She should've known he'd be able to cook. Rico D'Alessio would be good at most things. His pride demanded it.

"Well, for now there's no choice. I've cooked. You can eat it or starve."

"Shoving a frozen lump of cardboard in the oven does not constitute cooking," he growled.

"I'll leave it to you to show me what does constitute cooking," she said sweetly. "I've always enjoyed watching cooking programs, now I'll have my very own naked chef in my kitchen."

He shot her a glare that she suspected was designed to incinerate her on the spot. Danielle watched him fork the first mouthful of the lasagne into his mouth, pause and chew, a look of surprise on his face.

"Edible?"

He nodded. "Not half as bad as I expected. But if my mother heard me she'd disown me."

"Your mother…she lives in Italy, right?" With his younger sister, she remembered him saying.

Another nod.

"So how did you end up in New Zealand?"

He shrugged. "I did a stint in the SAS, and while stationed

in Afghanistan I met some members of the New Zealand SAS who sold me on their country. I came for a visit, met Lucia. Time came to leave I chose to stay. Next thing I knew I was married, and someone introduced me to your father and I had a job. That's the story of my life."

"Right!" She didn't believe him for an instant.

Rico was a jigsaw puzzle. A fascinating one. She had some pieces, but she still had a lot to put together.

After dinner he yawned and stretched. "Time to hit the sack."

Danielle stood, suddenly nervous. "You can go first. I've something I want to finish on my laptop, I'll be up shortly."

"Checking e-mail?"

"No!" Danielle shivered at the thought, knowing that Rico would demand to download her mail and check the messages first. The knowledge was oddly comforting. "I just want to give a report a final proofread." She didn't need to. But she wanted a reason to delay going to bed. If she could, she'd procrastinate until he was asleep.

"Okay, I'll keep you company."

Damn. She didn't want Rico hanging around but gave in. "I'll bring my laptop upstairs." It would give her an excuse to look busy in the lag of time before plunging the room into the dark, simmering air of expectancy that made her quiver.

He followed her up the stairs and all of a sudden that electrifying silence was back.

After dumping the laptop on the new bed and grabbing her nightie, Danielle scuttled into the bathroom and locked the door behind her—not that she expected Rico to follow her. A deep breath stilled the nervous tremors that vibrated through her. Composed at last, she shucked off her clothes and stepped into the shower.

Afterward she dried off, changed into her silk nightie and

returned to the bedroom. Rico stood beside the window, a dark shape in the unlit room. He didn't turn at the sound of the door opening. "It's beautiful tonight—the moon is rich and full."

"Let me see." She moved across the room.

"Careful. Remember what I said. Never stand in the centre of the window. Stand to the side, use the curtains to shield you, it will blur the shape of your body, making it difficult to get a clean shot."

She eased in beside him. Outside the moon hung low over the shiny black sea, so swollen and full that Danielle could imagine reaching out to touch it. The glow outlined the ghostly volcanic cone of Rangitoto Island, and the beauty tugged her heartstrings.

"This is why I love it here. The natural beauty, the space around one. It's a slice of paradise. I've missed it." His voice dropped to a low, mesmerising hum. Danielle was conscious of the romance of the dark, humid night, of Rico's scent, and her heart kicked up a beat.

Deliberately she placed her fingertips on his arm. His flesh was firm and warm, and the connection made her tingle. "I'm glad—glad you're back."

Rico went very still. Finally he let out his breath, and the sound was loud in the quiet room. "It's been a long day. I need a shower. Try to catch some rest, hmm?"

She sagged at the snub. He might as well have said, "Make sure you're asleep when I return, because I don't want to be bothered."

# Seven

"What's this?" she asked Rico the following Saturday morning. Fear knotted her stomach as she remembered the contents of the last envelope he'd handed her.

"Relax." His hand closed over hers.

Curious, she took the envelope and drew out a plastic folder embossed with a banking crest. Inside lay a wad of bank notes, a chequebook, a gold credit card and some promotional booklets. She stared at the innocuous items as though she'd discovered a pit of serpents.

She forced herself to reach out and pick up the credit card.

"Danielle D'Alessio." Would her heart always contract at the sight of that name? She ran her thumb over the raised print on the gold card and thought of the pile of plastic in her purse—and the invisible strings of control that went with them. She raised her gaze and said levelly, "I don't want these."

Instantly his brows met. "Why not? You're my wife."

Was that annoyance and…hurt…that lit his eyes? No, impossible! Nothing she could do would ever hurt Rico D'Alessio. "Your temporary wife—not your real wife!"

"We're married."

"Not for the reasons we should be." He'd certainly made his feelings for her clear—going to bed after she was already asleep, making sure he was out of the bedroom before she awoke. She hesitated, searching for the right words to explain how she felt. "But even if we were, I don't think I could take them."

His eyes went black. "I don't understand you."

"Well, you should!"

His head jerked back as if she'd slapped him. "What the hell is that supposed to mean?"

"You told me you didn't want your wife's money when she was alive, that you wanted to make it your own way. You had pride." She drew herself up to the full height of her five foot six inches. "Well, I have my pride, too—I need to establish my independence." Hurriedly she pushed the card, the cash and the brochures back into the folder and shoved it into his hands. "My father's always given me whatever I want. But there's always been a heavy price attached."

"And you think I would do the same? Use money as a hold over you?" He sounded affronted.

She took in his wounded expression, the way his bottom lip jutted out, and almost snorted. He looked like a little boy who'd been royally told off instead of a man who had her wedged between a rock and a hard place. She arched an eyebrow. "Wouldn't you?"

"Never!"

At his adamant response, she did snort. "Let's just say you have enough holds over me already."

He went silent, staring at the folder. When he finally looked up, his eyes were cool, all hint of the boyish appeal gone. "Look at it from my perspective. I'm staying in your house. You've stocked it with supplies, arranged for Parsons to order furniture. I don't pay rent. I'm essentially a kept man. This—" he shook the bank pack at her "—makes *me* feel better."

Kept man? His pride wouldn't like that. A smile tugged at the corners of her mouth. "I can see your dilemma. First, you offer to be my naked chef, and now it's almost like you're barefoot and pregnant in my kitchen."

He shot her a killing look.

She held up her hands. "Joke."

"Not funny."

"Oh, come on, Rico!"

He gave her a reproving glance. "You have a very wicked sense of humour. I'm not sure that I approve of you poking fun at me like this."

"Doesn't anyone ever laugh at you? Just a little?"

He managed to look both injured and insulted. Danielle stifled a smile. Tipping her head sideways, she considered the red slash of colour high on his cheekbones. "They don't, do they?"

"No, I'm the eldest," he said, the words sounding forced from him.

"Ah."

"Ah? What does this 'ah' mean?"

"And you're the only son. No wonder you take yourself too seriously. It's time for you to cut loose and have some fun, Rico."

He looked suspicious. "It's been a while since I've wanted to have fun."

Four years, at least, she thought, and her heart softened. After a moment's consideration, she said, "I tell you what, we'll compromise. You keep the chequebook and the cash. I'll take the card and I'll use it each month up to a limit, like rent. Okay?" She named a figure.

He looked like he was going to argue.

She upped the amount a little, hoping it would be enough to satisfy his masculine pride. But she refused to accept anything that could be construed as charity—or worse, an amount that he could later claim payback on. "And that's final."

"A stubborn streak lurks under your sweet exterior." His voice was curiously gentle. He opened the folder, extracted the money and pocketed it, then handed her the square of gold. Carelessly he dropped the folder on the table. "But today I'm going to be equally determined. I want to buy something for the house."

Danielle slowly nodded. If he could compromise—which she doubted had been an easy task for him—then so could she.

Saturday passed in a flash.

Back from Newmarket, Auckland's shopping Mecca, Rico admitted that he'd had fun. Fun when Danielle had dragged him into the seventh carpet shop and they'd found the perfect rug for the sitting room; when she'd selected a couple of ceramic planters with bright designs and when he'd found an ancient oak table that reminded him of the huge table in his parents' kitchen. The table where his mother pored over recipes, where he and his sisters had done their homework, and where his father spread his evening newspaper out. The kind of table that spelt generations.

Arriving home, he'd checked out the townhouse and then Danielle walked in, parcels rustling and the floaty fabric of her dress swirling around her. She reached the sitting room, kicked off her shoes, and collapsed onto the couch among an armful of packages.

"My feet are killing me," she said, laughing at him, as he returned pretending to stagger under the weight of more bags.

"Woman, never let it be said that you can't shop." He pulled a face at her. "Now, can I fix you a drink?"

"Something long and cool, please."

"Your wish is my command."

She flung her head back and, glancing sideways at him through crinkled, laughing eyes, she said, "Yeah, right!"

For a moment he was struck dumb by her vitality and joy. He could become addicted to the sound of her laughter. He shook himself free of the odd notion, like a dog ridding itself of rain, and strode quickly to the kitchen.

Minutes later he handed her a tall glass filled with a rich melon-coloured liquid. "Try this." He dropped down beside her, and his thigh brushed hers, the warmth of her body providing a connection that he found oddly comforting. Barely aware of his actions, her reached for her free hand, enfolding it his larger one.

"Lovely," she sighed, after a long sip. "Tell me about Lucia. How did you meet?"

He was so mellow, he barely flinched at the sudden question. "At an embassy function. I was there advising on security, she was there with a friend. She was Italian, it drew us together. I asked her out, she accepted. By the time I figured out who she was, it was too late."

He paused, remembering the argument he'd had with Lucia when he'd learned she was a member of the wealthy Ravaldi family. Pride smarting, he'd demanded to break it off, but she'd refused, insisting that they were in love, that she wanted to get married. Beautiful, tempestuous Lucia whom he'd loved to death.

"We were married within six weeks of our first meeting. Her family flew out for the wedding. But—" he shot Danielle

a wry look "—as you know, I'm a proud man. I was determined to stay in New Zealand and carry on working. My wife
wasn't going to support me. Sometimes my resolve annoyed
Lucia immensely." In the end they'd compromised. She used
her funds for clothes and other female fripperies, but they'd
lived simply in the apartment he'd rented, eating food he
bought.

"You were already married when you came to work for
Daddy. You must both have been very young."

"I was twenty-one when I met Lucia. She was eight years
older. I was stunned that this sophisticated woman of the world
found me so riveting." He gave a self-deprecating grin, remembering how flattered he'd been.

Danielle's face held an unfathomable expression. "I'm not
at all surprised that you snagged her attention." Then a wicked
gleam lit her eyes, and instantly her features were transformed.
"Even if you were only a baby."

"Baby?" Rico tried to sound affronted, but her sparkling
eyes made it impossible. "Who's the baby? I was only a year or
so younger than you are now." He smiled at her, and when she
grinned back, he suddenly felt on top of the world. Affection for
her warmed him. It had been so long since he'd spoken to anyone
about Lucia, it was as if a huge dam had broken inside him,
easing some inexplicable tension that he'd barely known existed.

With her free hand Danielle reached for her glass. Rico
watched her throat move as she swallowed the juice. He
followed the path of the liquid down to where the neckline of
the dress dropped in a sharp vee, to where the first of a row of
buttons nestled. Consciously he forced himself to relax his grip
on her slim fingers as the tension escalated inside him.

The fabric moulded her breasts—

He snapped his gaze away. Okay, so she was attractive.
She was kind.

And considerate.

And nice.

Finally he gave up cataloguing her virtues and simply admitted that he liked her, that he'd had a great day, that he'd had fun—maybe for the first time in years.

And that worried him.

Because this wasn't about enjoying himself. He'd set himself a task. One that he would never accomplish if he continued to allow guilt to gnaw his gut each time Danielle roused a smile. What he had to do was about more than revenge.

His father might be dying. He, Rico, was the last D'Alessio. He'd promised his father, at the high-sided hospital cot that he'd feared would be his father's deathbed, that he'd see to it.

Danielle Sinclair was going to provide him with a baby, an heir to the D'Alessio name. He couldn't allow the feeling that he was betraying Lucia to keep getting in the way. He'd loved Lucia. He'd *never* fall in love with Danielle Sinclair. No threat of betrayal to Lucia existed. This was about life—new life— not a new love. And he was avenging Lucia, too. Simple.

So when had it all become so complicated? Was it when he'd stood beside Danielle at that scarily real, fake wedding? When he'd held her fragile fingers in his, and vowed to love, cherish and honour *her?*

He tightened his hand around hers, and she twisted her fingers, lacing them through his. They fitted, warm and supple, against his.

Something stirred inside him.

Lust, he told himself. Nothing to feel furtive or guilty about. It was the age-old, primitive response of a red-blooded man to a beautiful woman he knew he was going to bed. Its strength came from the fact that it had been a long time since he'd been laid—it certainly would never impact his heart.

No one expected him to live like a monk.

He could do this. He *had* to do this.
Unless he was prepared to disappoint his father.

Danielle flexed her feet, stretching the arch that was tender from pounding the Newmarket pavements. Rico stood and she felt a sharp sense of loss as she watched him walk away through the archway. They'd shared laughter and a sense of kinship today. Now he was leaving her alone. All the happiness went out of her, like a deflated balloon.

It was dangerous to allow herself to be so happy. This was all temporary. She was staring blindly at her bare feet when Rico returned holding a towel she'd placed in the guest bathroom.

"Feet sore?" he asked as he sank down beside her.

"Killing me," she said. "What are you doing?"

"Can't have you limping around, so I'll have to make it better."

He stretched past her, and she caught his warm scent. Renewed hope stirred. Firmly she suppressed it. She could not allow herself to become hooked on Rico. Soon he'd be gone.

She pushed the disheartening thought away as he gently lifted her foot onto his lap and wrapped the hot, dampened towel around it. Oh, sheer bliss. Shutting her eyes, she focused on the heat penetrating her sore foot muscles and slowly relaxed. After a few minutes he pulled the towel free and deftly wrapped her other foot. Taking the freed foot between his hands, he started rubbing the arch, his thumb finding the knots and easing the aches.

Danielle moaned. "That is so good."

"Relax. Let the tension go." His fingers massaged the tender skin under her feet.

Danielle let her breath ease out. "Whatever you say."

He snorted. "Since when do you do what I want, hmm?"

"All the time." She smiled at him. "Rub my feet and I'll be your slave for life, oh master."

Rico made a choking sound. The eyes that met hers glinted with laughter. "I have never met a woman like you, who looks so biddable, yet underneath lies a will of pure steel."

"Oh." But his words flattered her. Here was someone who didn't consider her a dutiful daughter, a gullible sister, a doormat. No, she reminded herself sharply before the tide of emotion could spread the gentle warmth any further, to him she was simply a body to impregnate.

"Just when I think I know what to expect from you, you confound me." He switched feet, carefully lowering the first to the ground and firmly grasping the other. Then he gave it the same relentless attention. And she surrendered to the shivers of pain-edged pleasure that rippled upward from her feet as he tended to the kinks. She tipped her head back and sighed in ecstasy. "Mmm."

Slowly his hands followed the ripples in lazy arcs, up her calf…up…to the soft skin inside her knees. "Take what we're doing now. I'm rubbing your sore feet. You should be groaning with pain, yet you confound me, uttering those little murmurs of pleasure that make me grow hard."

Her pulse began to hammer. She made him hard. *He wanted her.*

The lowest button of the button-through dress gave. "Your skin feels warm and soft under my fingers." His thumb stroked across her thigh, and instantly her body turned to fire.

A second button slid free. She held her breath, waiting for his next move.

He shifted. "Danielle…"

When she opened her eyes, his face was above hers. So close that she could see his dilated pupils against the midnight irises.

"Yes?"

"Are you ready for this?"

She nodded. But a shard of doubt pierced her. Could she let Rico make love to her, knowing that all he wanted was her fertility? His hip brushed hers, and a bolt of heat leaped through her. He was hard and warm and male. Of course she could do this!

A frown creased his forehead. "Are you certain, *cara?*"

Her pulse thudded at the endearment. But then reality kicked in. He was simply trying to make it easier for both of them. It didn't mean a thing. For an instant she hesitated. Clinically she analysed her dilemma. She wanted Rico to show her what passion was all about. If she turned him down, told him everything…would he ever make a move on her again? Or would he simply write her off, walk away and find another woman? Perhaps even pursue Kim. She closed her eyes. "Yes, I'm certain."

A muscled arm slid under her back, the other under her knees. She felt her stomach lurch as he hoisted her up. "Rico!" She clutched at his shoulders. "What are you doing?"

"It must have been almost as long a time for you as for me if you need to ask that." He raised a brow at her and headed for the stairs. "I'm taking you somewhere more comfortable."

She slid her eyes away from his and bit her lip. By the time he reached the top of the stairs his heart drummed against her shoulder. Danielle suspected the rapid beat had more to do with anticipation than with exertion, and her own pulse quickened in response.

"I'd almost forgotten how good it feels to hold a woman. How soft you are," Rico said breathily against the side of her throat causing another wave of shivers to ripple through her.

She nuzzled her cheek against his hair, took a deep breath, steeling herself for what was to come, half wishing that she was better equipped to deal with it. All too soon, he laid her on the bedcover. For an instant their eyes met. He must've seen something in hers that revealed how much she craved this, because he groaned, and followed her down. Then his arms were around her and his lips came down on hers.

Instantly she was transported to that swirling void where nothing mattered except the taste of Rico, the feel of his hard body against hers. None of the doubts or uncertainties that had plagued her only minutes before had a place here.

There was only heat, adrenaline…and Rico.

He eased the dress away and his hand smoothed across her bare stomach. Her muscles trembled under his touch. Intense splinters of sensation followed in the wake of his fingers. As they brushed the base of her breasts, she gasped. A moment later the last button sprang free. The dress fell away from her body, leaving her clad only in a set of matching lacy bra and briefs.

Silently Danielle thanked the fact that she always wore exquisitely feminine snowy white underwear. Then the feminine thought was forgotten as his hand cupped her breast and a spasm of desire shot through her. She squeezed her eyes shut, focusing on each movement he made, each reaction that followed, glorying in the way her body responded to his touch.

There was nothing wrong with her. She wasn't frigid. The hurtful rumours that labelled her Ice Queen were untrue.

The realisation liberated her. She hungered to touch him, as he was touching her. She tugged at his cotton shirt, pulling it free from the waistband of his jeans. Rico lifted his upper body and, with one impatient shrug, whipped the shirt off.

Her breath caught at the sight of his bare chest with its dusting of dark hair. She lifted her fingers to trace the muscle definition of his pectorals, and he responded with a shudder that expanded the magnificent chest under her fingertips. Instantly she increased the pressure of her fingers, loving the feel of his skin, the tension that vibrated through his big body.

He sat up. She heard the rasp of his zipper, and apprehension blossomed inside her. He pushed his jeans down and kicked them away. Only a pair of black briefs remained. Her gaze rested on the betraying bulge. The apprehension escalated to a nervous anxiety. This was the point of no return. After his briefs came off there was no going back.

Before she could express her hesitation, he'd rolled back and swept her close, his lips claiming hers again. The feel of his nearly naked body against her bare skin caused shivers to ripple through her, until her teeth started to clatter from a combination of tightly leashed nerves and excitement.

He pulled back. "Cold?"

She swallowed and shook her head.

"Scared?"

"A little," she answered honestly.

"Of me?" He lifted his hand away, his eyes troubled. "Why?"

There was no honest answer that she could give him.

Clumsily Danielle grabbed his hand and pressed his palm against her heart. "And excited, too," she added quickly. It was true. Trepidation and anticipation warred inside her, her heartbeat quickening under the weight of his hand.

His gaze ignited. "You have no idea how that makes me feel."

At his ragged comment, the first surge of confidence filled her. *She could do this*. It wasn't going to be nearly as difficult as she'd anticipated.

His fingers slid along the upper curve of her breast, under the edge of lace. An instant later her bra gave way. Danielle arched up as he stroked her breast, a guttural sound breaking from her throat.

"I want to kiss you here."

She nodded fervently, then tensed as his head lowered, expecting him to touch the painfully sensitive nipples. Instead, he tongued the underside of her breast, awakening undiscovered pleasure. She flung her head back and waited breathlessly for his next move. When it came, she shuddered and let out a wild keening sound.

"Oh, Rico!"

He lifted his head, his eyes smouldering. "Good?"

"Fantastic!"

She wanted to tell him not to stop, but shyness overwhelmed her. Seconds later his tongue trailed around the rosy tip and more of the unexpectedly intense pleasure shot through her.

The muscles in her abdomen contracted as she fought the wave of shivers that threatened to overtake her, the newness of it all dissolving her flesh into a substance resembling jelly. Adrenaline pounded through her, edged with nervous energy, and her heart raced.

Rico's mouth traced down between her breasts, paused for a moment to plant a kiss over her belly button, then continued. His thumbs hooked under the sides of her panties, she felt them give. Excitement and apprehension pounded through her, and she waited for his next sensual assault.

But instead of stripping off her panties he paused, and raised his head. His fingers hovered above her belly.

She knew what he'd seen. Despairingly, she shut her eyes.

"These are from the accident, aren't they?"

She stilled, but his fingertips mercifully failed to touch the ridged tissue. "Yes." Her lashes lay against her cheeks, delicate crescent shaped shadows against her skin.

"I'm sorry," he said brusquely.

"It was a long time ago."

"But it still hurts."

She suspected he wasn't talking about the barely noticeable silvery lines, which were more pronounced to touch than to the eye. She thought about her mother, about her unfulfilled dreams, her longings that had died in the aftermath of the accident.

A pause. "Yes."

He moved away.

She felt suddenly chilled. This was it. This was where he'd look at her with pity in his eyes and tell her that it was over.

"See this?"

Astonished, she stared at him. He hadn't withdrawn, and although she couldn't see his eyes, he didn't sound like a man who was about to walk away. He was still here, lying full length beside her. Hope fluttered perilously within her.

"Here," he said, pointing to his right side.

She bent over his stomach to look, her eyes lingering on the flat, muscled expanse of flesh. A mark, only a couple of inches long, marred the perfection of his smooth, tanned skin.

"You've got a scar, too." But the small mark couldn't be anywhere near as traumatic as the memories that impaired her.

"Glass. I got it the day your mother died." The eyes that met hers were clouded. "I walked away with a couple of shards of glass in me. If your mother had been sitting where I was, that's all she would've suffered."

"Rico," she said, shaken. "*It was an accident.* My mother died as a result of some drunk's recklessness. Nothing you could've done would've prevented it."

His hand stroked along her ribs, his touch so gentle that her throat thickened painfully.

"We switched seats, she wanted to sit in the front passenger seat. It should've been me that died. Instead I walked free and your mother died, Jim was severely injured and your emotional wounds affected you for years."

It was a long time since she'd heard Jim Dembo's name mentioned. Jim had been driving that fateful day. He'd been injured, concussed. He'd never fully recovered from his injuries, never been able to work again.

She sighed; three lives affected by one man's criminal carelessness. She glanced at Rico. It wasn't only she, Jim and her mother who'd been affected. Rico, too, bore the mark of that day.

Hooking an arm around his shoulders, she said, "You feel responsible—guilty!"

He shifted his gaze, and she watched the dark tide of colour flush his skin. He remained silent. She set him at arm's length and glared. "Now that is ridiculous. *It's not your fault.*"

"Your mother died. You were trapped in that wreck for hours." His voice grew hoarse, until he finally looked away. "Hell. For months afterwards you were as silent as a ghost."

Memories of his gentle smiles, of how he'd gone out of his way to talk to her assailed her. And now she knew why.

*Oh, no.* Still holding him away, Danielle dropped her head. She'd mistaken his guilt and concern for something else, something that had made her listless, aching heart quicken at the sound of his longed-for voice.

She'd thought he'd noticed that she was growing up, becoming a woman.

All he'd been offering was compassion, a shoulder to cry on. Not love, not arms to hold her. It had been pity for a motherless girl. Pity because he had some stubborn notion that he was partly responsible for her mother's tragic death.

She'd been a silly little fool.

But it was different now. This time he needed her. For an heir. Heck, did it really matter why he needed her? It was enough that he did. She forced her hands to relax, loosening her grip, she trailed her fingers down the inside of his elbow. "We're talking too much."

He gave her a sharp glance. "Should I kiss you instead?"

"Please," she said huskily, and pulled him towards her.

His lips were gentle. And she responded like a blossom to the sun with the promise of a fruitful summer to come. Danielle sighed and lay back, barely noticing the brush of the Egyptian cotton against her back, aware only of Rico's naked body lying against hers.

Slowly his hands resumed the long strokes over her body, fanning the flames that had subsided, until the heat built to an unbearable point. His leg glided over hers and the weight of his solid thigh made her wriggle.

"Too heavy?"

"No!" Couldn't he understand? She wanted more. She wanted him to cover her, his whole weight plastered against her body. She tugged.

He slid over her, his skin smooth and warm against hers. Under his warm heaviness, she moaned. This was what she craved. He fitted against her like he belonged. Like she'd come home.

It was at once comforting and arousing.

She could feel his erection straining against her. Restlessly she parted her legs, and he shifted, jigsawing against her, their underwear providing the only barrier. She moved, and he butted her in response. Again she drove her hips upward, and this time he groaned in response.

"You're killing me. Slowly but surely, you're killing me," he muttered against the curve of her neck.

Danielle twisted wildly against him, not sure where this was going, but comfortable that her body seemed to know what it was doing.

His mouth opened on the soft skin of her neck. Her breath

stopped as wave after wave of sensation coursed across her nape. Another wriggle, and then a thrill shot through her as his lower body pressed inexorably against hers.

For a moment he pulled away, his hands smoothing down her legs. Then he was back, and for the first time his complete nakedness met her soft moistness, their briefs gone.

For a fleeting instant panic engulfed her.

*What if she was making a mistake?* Then a calm sense of purpose descended on her. She wanted this. *She wanted Rico.*

She let him nudge her thighs apart, until his length rested intimately against her. He shifted. Then his slick fingers were against her, touching her. Embarrassment shocked through her. But it gave way to heat as a sensation she'd never experienced quivered through the sensitised skin.

Hesitantly she let him have more access.

He took it. Pulses of excitement centred around her core, as she built towards some driving completion she'd never experienced. She thrashed under him, not sure what to do to reach the burning summit she sought.

"Slow down, we'll get there."

She shoved her hand down, curled it around him. His chest rose against her. She heard his gasp.

"Slowly! I haven't done this in a while." It sounded like he was gritting his teeth. Joy overwhelmed her. He *did* want her. She was giving him the same pleasure that streaked like silver flames through her.

Awkwardly she moved her hand up and down, felt the pressure as his hips pressed down. Delicately she bit the side of his neck, tasted the dewy salt on his skin and licked gently. His big body shuddered.

The blunt pressure increased. She felt her body give, felt him slip through the gateway. Her breath caught in surprise. He was big, stretching her tight.

\* \* \*

Rico's mouth closed over her parted lips, the kiss desperate and hungry.

Even as he kissed her, Rico felt her hesitation. She'd stopped those little rocking moves that had driven him wild. She seemed to be waiting.

Did she want him to hurry up? Immediately, he sank deep into her. Underneath him she jerked. Perhaps she was hotter than he realised. He sped up; she gasped under his mouth, but her hips remained still. Confusion tore at him. He pulled his head up. "Am I hurting you?"

The lake-gray eyes were uncertain, a little bewildered. No sign of her usual cool confidence. She gave her head a little shake.

He frowned.

"I'm fine. Don't stop."

He started to pull out of her. To try something different.

"No!" Her arms closed around him, tugging him back. "Please, don't stop. I couldn't bear it if you left me now."

Rico slid home and gave a harsh groan as her knees parted and twined up around him, increasing the fit. "Oh, no. I can't hold back anymore."

His body went into overdrive, even as he fought for control, tried to slow down, to prolong the pleasure. But it was too late.

Burying his face against her neck, he murmured incoherently and then frantically kissed the soft skin with raw hunger. The beat of his blood roared in his ears, and he gritted his teeth as he battled to hold off the waves of gratification.

"Aah!" He squeezed his eyes shut as satisfaction claimed him in spurts of pleasure. "I'm sorry," he choked. "Next time will be for you, I promise."

"Next time?"

He raised his head. She was quite still under him, her eyes puzzled.

"Shouldn't be long. You make me feel like a kid again."

"Now?"

He stared at her, trying to put his finger on exactly what was bothering him. "Maybe not right now." He gave a lopsided smile. "I'm not a super hero, but given the effect you have on me, I don't doubt it will be soon."

She smiled back—a little wavering—but a smile nonetheless. A muscle near his heart contracted. "Or I can finish you now, if you don't want to wait?"

"Finish me?"

He frowned. Was this for real? Had no man ever given her an orgasm?

"Hey, what kind of men do you associate with?"

Caution glinted in her eyes. "What do you mean?"

"Haven't you ever…you know…" He shrugged, felt his face start to burn.

Her gaze flickered. Then her mouth firmed. "No, I've never…you know…"

At the stilted way she parroted his words back at him a wave of gentle affection swept over him. He'd sort that out. Teach her what being a woman was about.

More strongly she added. "This was the first time."

*The first time?* Her words yanked him back. She *had* to be talking about orgasms, meaning that she'd never had one before. She couldn't possibly mean…

He stared disbelievingly into her cool, pale face. He remembered her hesitation. The waiting, the soft butterfly touches, the clumsy hands, the shivering. Hardly the actions of an experienced woman who knew the score.

Horror engulfed him as the puzzle crystallised. It *had* been her first time.

*Danielle Sinclair had been a virgin.*

# Eight

"I didn't know." Sitting on the edge of the bed, his head in his hands, Rico sounded as if she'd accused him of some crime. Regret and remorse radiated from every line of his naked body. "I honestly didn't know."

"You couldn't have known. I never told you," Danielle said in her most composed voice, almost wishing she could regret what they'd shared. It would've made his humiliating reaction easier to cope with. But she couldn't. In fact, she could barely wait for it to happen all over again, that tug of longing...the heat...and the splendid shimmering pleasure. She suspected there was a lot more still to discover, and she had no doubt that Rico would know exactly what to teach her.

His head shot up. "Why?"

"Why what?" She answered his question with another.

"Don't play word games with me, damn it! Okay, so you'd

found it hard to tell me something so intimate. But what I can't understand…" He shook his head, clearly at a loss. Then, meeting her gaze, he said, "You're how old?"

"Twenty-two," she answered promptly.

"I know that," he growled.

At his irritation, she fought the small smile that threatened. "But you asked."

"It was a rhetorical question. Believe me, I know how old my wife is!"

He'd called *her* his wife. For the first time since he'd pulled away, her spirits lifted. She stretched, her limbs still tingled, and the sheet slipped, revealing the curve of her breast.

He glared at her. "How does a twenty-two-year-old get to stay a virgin in today's society?"

"Is that also a rhetorical question?" she asked demurely.

"No," he said. "This time I want an answer."

"Lack of opportunity."

*"Lack of opportunity?"* He looked flummoxed. "That's all you can come up with?"

"You try doing anything with your father breathing down your neck, staff reporting your every movement."

"It didn't seem to inhibit Kimberly."

"Kim's an exhibitionist, she didn't mind everyone know *exactly* what she was up to. I wanted privacy." And something more.

"But what about all those university boys?"

Boys. That was exactly what they'd been. "They were too young."

"What about the men at work? They're not young."

"You've seen them. Most are married—or too old."

"Too young, too old." Rico looked nonplussed.

He made her sound fussy, like she'd been waiting for Mr. Right. She shifted, uncomfortable with where this was going.

Rico's gaze dropped and she realised that the sheet had slipped another inch.

She refused to hike it up like…like some outraged virgin. He could look as much as he wanted. Defiantly she let it slide another inch.

Swiftly his eyes jerked back to hers, his cheekbones awash with colour, his heavy-lidded gaze holding a shocked question.

At least she knew he still wanted her. Satisfaction curled through her. But the uncertainty clouding his features astonished her. Rico obviously thought she wouldn't want to repeat the experience. Surely it couldn't have been *that* bad? In fact, she'd thought it pretty marvellous, until it had ended so abruptly.

She drew in a deep breath, searching for words that might make him understand. "There comes a time when it's hard to admit you're…inexperienced. What was I supposed to do? Walk up to some stranger and say, 'Please help me. I want to get laid, but I've never done it before, so you'll need to go real slow and show me what to do'?"

His dark-chocolate eyes turned black, the fleeting vulnerability gone. "Don't be stupid!" he snarled in a voice as sharp as a whip.

"I'm not. I'm trying to make you understand my dilemma."

"Except I didn't go real slow, I rushed you." Rico groaned, and raked his hands through his hair. "Hell. Did you have to choose me to solve your dilemma?"

That hurt. "If you remember, I didn't have much choice at all," she pointed out. "You threatened to break up my sister's marriage, if I didn't do what you wanted."

He looked shaken. "I didn't think you'd be a—"

"You didn't think!" Danielle sat up, uncaring that the sheet dropped away as she jabbed a finger at his chest. "That's your problem, you plotted this elaborate scheme, but you never thought about it. Not really. Not about who you might hurt, what the consequences might be."

He flinched. "I didn't expect you to be an innocent." His gaze slipped down, before he wrenched it back to her face, the flush restaining his cheekbones.

She straightened her back, her breasts full and pert, and watched with satisfaction as Rico sneaked another look. "Well, I am. I'm innocent of everything—except being a Sinclair."

"Danielle—"

She interrupted him. "I don't understand why you're making such a big thing of this, anyway. My virginity won't stand in the way of what you want."

"Not anymore." He sounded strange. "You accomplished that much. But don't underplay its importance." At last his annoyance seemed to be receding. If she didn't know better she would've pegged his expression as a little smug. "I don't think I've ever made love to a virgin in my life. That's what blew me away. It's something you should've kept for your husband, seeing that you've abstained for so long."

"You *are* my husband," she pointed out, irritated that she needed to remind him. Then she thought about what she'd revealed and backtracked, in case he started to put it together, in case he realised that he'd been the only man she'd ever desired. "And that's such an old-fashioned view to take, it makes you sound like a dinosaur."

"A dinosaur?"

"Yes, one of those monstrous creatures that lived millions of years ago."

"Are you comparing me to Tyrannosaurus Rex?" He raised a brow, and a ghost of laughter gleamed in his eyes. "I'm no dinosaur—I'm simply Italian."

*Oh, Rico.* She started to laugh, even as she turned to mush. With his dishevelled hair, and the inky lock that had fallen over his forehead again, she wanted to throw herself into his arms, kiss him and start all over again. Which made her wonder...

"I hope that this...peculiar...reaction of yours to my untouched state doesn't mean that you've been overcome with scruples?"

At her words his brows drew into a thick black line. "Meaning?"

"We will do this again, won't we?"

He hesitated, glancing away. When he looked back the laughter had gone, and his eyes were sombre, unfathomable. "We shouldn't. If I had a grain of honour, we wouldn't. But somehow, I don't think I could stop myself if I tried."

"Good," she said with simple complacency and leaned towards him. "Now can we try it again? Perhaps a little slower this time?"


"Satisfied?" Rico propped himself up on an elbow and smiled at the woman curled against him.

"Oh, yes!" Her emphatic reply made him laugh. A hectic flush lay across her cheeks, and her awed gaze made him feel like a man who could conquer mountains of gigantic proportions. His discomfort at his rather inadequate earlier performance had vanished, leaving him feeling rather pleased with himself. Rico suspected somewhere down the line his conscience was going to kick in, and he was going feel shame. At taking her innocence, at involving her—

No! He would deal with his conscience and the consequences of his actions when it was all over. When he held his son in his arms.

"At least now I know that I'm not...cold."

Abandoning his concerns about his conscience, he paid attention to what she was saying and frowned. "You're not cold. You're one of the warmest, happiest people I know."

"I'm not talking about that."

"Then what are you talking about?"

"Sex," she replied succinctly.

"Sex?" Then the penny dropped, and he added in disbelief, "You thought you were sexually cold?" Rico started to laugh again. "You thought you were *frigid?*"

"It's not funny!"

He stopped grinning. The truculence in her face told him she was serious. "Sorry. Perhaps your odd sense of humour is starting to rub off on me."

"Please, don't laugh about this. I'm sensitive about it."

Her lake-calm eyes held that vulnerable expression that always caused a constriction in his chest. "So I see. But why? Where did you get such an incredibly ridiculous notion?"

A thought struck him. One that he found he didn't care for. Not a bit. Even though he suspected it was unreasonable. "Did you have a relationship with someone who told you were frigid? Or, perhaps, you shared a little…intimacy…and he made you believe you were cold?"

"No! Nothing like that." She stared ahead.

The relief that filled him was out of proportion. He shouldn't be feeling like this. The thought of Danielle with some other man should be of no interest to him. But he was interested.

*Because she was his.*

The surge of possessiveness astounded him. Not sure whether he liked it, or what it might signify, he shoved it out of sight to analyse later.

"I overheard some guys talking about me at university. One said I was a frigid little witch."

Anger rose in Rico. *Jerk.* "Had he tried to score with you?"

"No, he'd asked me out. But I refused because I didn't date boys in my class. I didn't want to deal with the post-breakup fallout every day."

"That's your answer. He was a scorned man."

"But the others round him all agreed. They barely knew me."

"So why let yourself be affected by a judgement made by a group of stupid jerks whose sole interest was in getting laid? Especially when it's so patently untrue?"

"I thought…" She coloured.

"You thought…?" He urged her on, intrigued by this complex, wholly feminine woman.

She turned her head. "I thought maybe it was obvious to anyone who cared to look."

Rico admired the straight nose, the revealing up-tilted chin. "Evident that you were frigid?" he asked in disbelief.

The rosy colour on her cheeks deepened. "It sounds ridiculous."

"Frigidity isn't a label you wear any more than virginity. Hell, I didn't even spot that, even though there were clues. Nor, I bet, did all your wannabe swains."

She gave a giggle and met his eyes. "Rico. A label. How absurd! Do I look like the type to walk around wearing a T-shirt proclaiming I Am a Virgin?"

"No. You don't look like anyone's idea of a virgin. Whatever that may look like." He splayed his fingers. "Nor would anyone believe a T-shirt that stated I'm Frigid." Rico stretched out a hand and gently traced her lips. "These full, soft lips promise passion and belie coldness." He reached the corner of her mouth. "The curve here shows humour, a zest for life, which aren't qualities that I'd associate with someone with a low sex drive."

His hand lingered.

"There's more. At work they call me the Ice Queen." She spoke through his fingers, her lashes lowered. "*You* even call me 'Princess.'"

He stroked his hand tenderly up the side of her face. "Yeah, but that's a joke between you and me. I say it when I'm trying to provoke a reaction out of you, ruffle your perfect feathers when you're at your most disdainful. Nothing more. And who cares about the rest of them? You're sweet and kind and generous…and frankly nothing else matters."

"Thank you, Rico." She rested her head on his chest and snuggled closer into the curve of his body.

Rico wrapped his arms around her, brushed a kiss over the top of her head and closed his eyes against the pain that tightened around his heart like an iron fist.

After taking her innocence, how could she thank him? When his eyes opened again, he stared blindly over her head, into a future that made his eyes grow dark.

The first month of marriage to Rico passed in a flash.

Danielle readily admitted that she couldn't keep her hands off Rico—and he seemed to have no compunction touching her, either. She'd been a little concerned after the first night that he would impose that awesome control and restrain himself, but he'd seemed to have decided that the damage was done.

She had no cause for complaint. Now that she'd finally discovered what all the fuss surrounding the topic of sex was about, Danielle decided that waiting for years had not detracted from the pleasure. In fact, it had made her curious, eager to learn more.

Apart from a few occasions when he became quiet and withdrawn, it had been easier than she'd ever expected to live with Rico. Much of the tough-guy machismo he presented to the world muted into warm protectiveness when he was alone with her. If it hadn't been for his constant reminders that she should remain watchful, that she was not yet safe because the stalker had not yet been apprehended, her life would've been idyllic.

And, if she was honest, the other thing that got to her was the dark place Rico escaped to when he went all silent. A place she couldn't follow because at those times he thought of *her*, his real wife—the reason for his crazy desire for revenge.

And then there was the discomfort of confessing to Rico that she wasn't pregnant. She felt even worse when a week later Rico had hugged her.

"Don't fret. The baby will come to us when it's meant to."

Baldly she'd asked him, "What if it's not meant and I don't get pregnant?"

He'd shrugged, seemingly unperturbed. "Give it time. It will happen soon enough."

Her fingers had twisted his shirt front. "You sound so certain."

The squeeze he gave her was intended to comfort. Danielle felt nothing but shame.

"I am," he said. "It'll take time for your body to recover from the cycle of the pill."

"I've never taken the pill," she pointed out. "I never needed it."

"Oh!" His eyes darkened to a shade that she recognised instantly and her pulse speeded up. His arms swept her up. "How could I ever forget."

His smile melted away her unease and his kiss heated her. "We'll simply have to try harder, practise more." Rico carried her back to the bedroom, and that had been the end of the discussion for the rest of the afternoon.

But the doubt-devils came back to plague her at odd moments, in the middle of a meal shared with Rico, during an interview she'd conducted for a Sinco post with a radiantly pregnant woman. When she and Rico got home that night her lovemaking was frenzied and intense, because Danielle knew her happiness was so ephemeral it was only a matter of time before the joy slipped from her grasp, however despairingly she clutched it to her heart.

And then she'd have only memories.

Three weeks later Danielle shut down her laptop and then glanced through Cynthia's office to where Rico sat in Martin's office and called, "All done for the day!"

He glanced up, and gave her one of those slow smiles that made her heart soften and turn to liquid. "Ready to roll, Princess?"

She nodded, her throat suddenly tight. How quickly she'd grown accustomed to his presence in her life. Soon Martin would be back from the three months paternity leave he'd taken, and Rico would be gone, shifted to the tenth floor, and the space across the room that he'd filled in the next office would be empty. The stalker was no longer enough of a reason for his presence. There'd been no sign of the man since their marriage. Rico's scare tactics had worked.

Danielle shifted on her chair, her lower back aching. She knew what event the ache signified, and she quailed at the news she'd have to break to Rico.

No baby. Not this month.

How much longer would he give her?

A movement caught her eye. Rico leaned against the doorjamb. The dark Italian suit accentuated his height, the male solidness of his body. She said the first thing that came into her head, "Have the police made any further headway identifying my crazy?"

The eyes that met hers were dark with frustration. "Nothing."

"So he's no longer a threat?"

"A stalker is always a threat." Rico rubbed his the dark stubble on his chin. "And this one is no fool. The longer he stays out of sight, the less priority the police assign to him."

Frustration boiled up inside her. She'd been so sure that the man had vanished, she'd started to relax. "Darn. So you don't think it's safe out there yet?"

Rico pushed away from the door and came round her desk to stand behind her. "Growing tired of me, Princess?"

Thankful that he couldn't see her face, the yearning for him to stay, she murmured, "Of course not."

The hard warmth of his hands on her shoulders steadied her. "Princess, I'll get him, if he tries anything, I promise you." His fingers stroked through her hair, rested on her nape and started to massage the tense knots there.

"Mmm." She sighed appreciatively and dropped her head forward. "What if it takes years and years?"

"You're too tense." His fingers found another knot. "Relax now, I've made you a promise."

"You'll grow tired of minding me."

"Well, there won't only be you, there'll be some bambinos, too."

"No, there won't." She knew she should let it go. But she couldn't. "One child—then you'll be gone."

The massaging hand paused. "Is that what's worrying you? I'd never leave you vulnerable. Even when you hand my son over, I'll protect you from harm."

Danielle's heart plummeted. Never had she been more aware of the sword of Damocles that hung constantly over her head. One slip and she was done for. Absently she shifted.

"Back ache?" Rico started to rub lower.

She nodded, loath to tell him why her back ached at this time of the month, hoping he'd figure it out for himself.

"Lean forward."

She folded her arms on the desk and lay forward, squeezing her eyes shut as his fingers tugged her blouse out of the waistband of her skirt. He slid his hands beneath the blouse and started to massage the muscles straddling her spine. Slowly the ache eased. If only all her problems could vanish beneath his touch. Flexing her shoulders, she straightened.

"Better?"

"Thank you." She barely heard him cross the room, his footfalls as silent as a large cat on the carpet as he left her office. A series of whirrs and clicks alerted her to the fact that he was shutting down his laptop. With a sigh she shrugged into her jacket and started to pack her bag, then she stopped, pulled her laptop back out and placed it back in the centre of her desk.

"Let's cut loose and go out to dinner tonight," she suggested rashly. She needed Rico's smile to rid her of the blue feeling that had plagued her all day. Telling herself that it was past that time of month, hadn't helped. She needed a lift. A night out with Rico would give her that. "I've had enough. All work and no play…will make Jill a very dull girl." She tossed him what she hoped looked like a careless grin.

"You could never be dull." He paused in the act of buttoning his jacket.

"Thanks, kind sir. But some days I sit here and think I'll be as grey as ditchwater."

Giving her a curious glance, he asked, "So why are you doing this?" His hand moved in an arc, embracing her workstation, the computer and the four corners of the office.

"Because I needed to finish my report."

Straightening his collar, he came into her office. "I mean why are you working here, at Sinco?" He perched himself on the edge of her desk. "Why do a business degree at all? I remember when you were a teenager you wanted to be a kindergarten teacher."

She glanced away and Rico knew her well enough now to know that she was avoiding his gaze. Then, her lips barely moving, she said, "What do goody-goody fifteen-year-olds know about careers?"

"Your mother thought it would suit you. I seem to remember her getting you some babysitting jobs with her friends."

"My father used to hit the roof at the thought of his daughter babysitting. He couldn't understand why I did it. After all, he gave me a generous allowance."

"Did your father stand in your way when the time came to study?"

She blinked but said nothing.

He tried another question. "Was he responsible for your change of careers?"

She shook her head. "No. I decided all by myself. I do have some original thoughts, you know."

Now she sounded put out. He hadn't meant to offend her. "Trust me, I do know." He tried to placate her, before returning to the topic he'd been pursuing. "But I remember that you loved kids. On the couple of occasions that David Matthews brought his kids, you always took them over, entertained them." He remembered her playing ball with the pair of towhead twins in the tropical gardens, to the horror of Henry, the gardener.

"In the end I decided to do something else with my life."

Her voice was calm, and Rico felt awkward making a big deal of something that was so obviously a nonevent. Danielle had simply grown up and turned her back on her teen dream. So why did he care? "I suppose." He shrugged and slid off the desk. "Well, one day you'll have your own kids to enjoy, so why run after other peoples' children, hmm?"

Her tight face alerted him. He thought over his words and wanted to groan at his lack of tact. She wouldn't have her own child because she'd contracted to give the baby up—to him.

Even though he'd told her that he'd stick around until her tormentor was caught, in reality he knew it wouldn't take years. Soon it would all be over; the man wouldn't stay out of sight much longer. Stalkers liked to terrify their victims, play with them and see the results of their actions.

Once she was safe, Rico knew he wouldn't be playing house with Danielle and a bunch of children. There'd be one child only. A child that he'd take, leaving her with an empty nest. He watched her with worried eyes. When he'd proposed the deal, it had been with Danielle Sinclair woman-of-the-world. Not the virginal waif he'd discovered.

He'd forgotten about her penchant for children.

Or had he? He frowned, drumming his fingers against his thigh. Had he subconsciously picked her because he knew she loved children? Because he wanted his child to be loved while it lay in her womb?

Another vivid fragment came back. Of the stoic pain she'd endured after she'd lost her mother. Would she be able to endure another loss? Or would it tip her over the edge into the turbulent vortex she'd inhabited as a teenager? What price would his revenge have on her when she had to surrender his child?

Troubled, he gazed at the woman he'd grown to…like. So intensely feminine, so desirable. But with a gentle kindness that soothed his tormented soul.

Abruptly he stopped drumming his fingers. For God's sake, what was he thinking? He had no choice; for the sake of his sanity and his family he had to go through with the plan. He tried to ignore the voice inside his head that insisted by taking her baby he would rip her heart out.

And suddenly he didn't much like the man he'd become.

# Nine

"To make-believe marriages."

Danielle glanced across the elaborately laid table to see how Rico would respond to her father's taunt. To her surprise, Rico merely smiled and raised the wineglass filled with the rich ruby liquid he'd been examining.

"To marriage," he toasted calmly.

Her father looked taken aback. Pride welled through Danielle. Bradley and Kim should've attended this first Sunday-evening family meal, too, but at the last minute Kim had cried off, leaving her and Rico as her father's sole guests. Glancing at Rico, Danielle couldn't help thinking how much her husband looked like an advertisement for *GQ* with his casually styled Armani suit, his hair falling over the back of the unbuttoned shirt collar. The familiar flare of physical attraction ignited as her gaze moved over him. Hurriedly, she turned her attention back to her father. "Rico's been helping me to furnish the townhouse."

"Trying your hand at interior design, D'Alessio? How interesting," Robert Sinclair drawled, and her hands curled into fists, until her nails bit into her palms.

"His name is Rico, Daddy. And it looks fabulous—you should come see."

"Not my style. As long as all this nest-making doesn't interfere with your work it's of little interest to me." Her father sounded bored. "How's the employee day care centre proposal getting on? Martin promised me a proposal—even though I'm not sure it's workable."

She stared at him blankly. Martin hadn't mentioned anything about it before he'd gone on paternity leave. Nor had she found any mention of anything similar in Martin's Outlook diary or in any of the files on his desk. He certainly hadn't brought it up when she'd called him about something else yesterday, although to be fair, she'd had other things on her mind, like the distressful arrival of her period a couple of days late and lighter than usual.

Perhaps he'd forgotten. She made a mental note to call Martin tomorrow and sort it out. She had no intention of sneaking on her boss to her father. Finally she asked, "When is his proposal due?"

"Don't you know? What's the matter with you, girl? Is playing house muddling your brain?" her father said, his voice heavy with impatience.

"That's uncalled for."

Danielle started as Rico spoke harshly from beside her.

"Ah, you're an expert on what my daughter does for my company?" Robert Sinclair raised an eyebrow. "You understand the finer points of human resource management?"

Danielle squirmed at the hostility that poured from her father's mouth. When her father discovered the truth—that they were *really* married and that the marriage had been consummated—there'd be hell to pay.

Rico leaned back in the Georgian chair and played with the stem of his wineglass. "Come down to the sixth floor any evening of the week and that's where you'll find your daughter. Working. Not playing house as you so quaintly put it. She's so terrified of a charge of nepotism being levelled against her that she works twice as hard as anyone else—and, yes, she's doing Dunstan's job in his absence as well."

The diamond-hard edge to Rico's voice gave her father reason to pause. Danielle watched with bated breath as the men traded stares. Her father gave way first. "Perhaps you should remind D'Al—Rico—" her father amended "—that I am your father, not the enemy. The enemy is the madman he's supposed to be apprehending before you get killed."

"He knows that, Daddy." Surreptitiously she placed a hand on Rico's thigh under the table. Muscle as tense as coiled steel moved under her fingers. Rico was nowhere near as relaxed as his appearance suggested.

"Trust me, Sinclair, your daughter will not end up dead, not while I have breath in my body." Rico's fierce words resonated with passion and made her heart soar. She turned to him, but he was watching her father, his hard, unyielding profile etched against the subtle lamplight that glowed on the antique table against the wall.

Her protector. Secure in Rico's presence beside her, she knew that her father's cruel words could not touch her. The uncompromising way in which Rico had confronted her father caused joy to flood her, and a sudden realisation struck her: what she felt for Rico was far more than desire.

It had to be love.

Shaken, she examined her discovery. It *couldn't* be love. It didn't resemble the gentle devotion she'd always expected love to be. It was too strong and stormy. And, like a tropical storm, she knew it would blow past leaving behind devastation and tears. Her tears.

Pushing her chair back, her stomach heaving, Danielle muttered an excuse.

Rico whirled around, the anger in his eyes rapidly sharpening to concern.

"Danielle…?"

She blinked furiously, determined he shouldn't see anything amiss. "Give me a few minutes, I need the bathroom." She desperately needed time to regain her composure. And to get the unexpected nausea that threatened to humiliate her under control. Through the pricking tears, she read the speculation on her father's face; she forced herself to slow down, to move with her usual calm grace.

The bathroom she took refuge in looked unfamiliar—even though she'd approved the décor that the sophisticated designer had selected. Looking around at the white-on-white colour scheme, at the mirrors and hard shiny surfaces, she decided that the sterile environment was definitely not to her taste, however prestigious the designer her father had appointed had been. And relief fluttered through her that she'd finally found the courage to leave her father's home. For too long he'd run her life and she'd allowed him to do it.

Rico had given her the opportunity to escape. And she wouldn't be back. As she turned the tap and let the cool water sluice into her hands, she thought of how sharing a home with Rico had given her some inkling of how other people lived, without a bevy of cleaners and cooks and chauffeurs around all the time.

Cupping her hands, she stared at the clear water pooling against her palms. Already the sick feeling in the pit of her stomach was subsiding. She'd make an appointment with the doctor this week, check if she was perhaps anaemic. Her last period had barely been more than spotting, and now this. Danielle bent forward and splashed her face. But anaemia was minor compared to the dilemma that now faced her.

When she raised her head to stare in the mirror she knew that she'd never regret loving Rico. Never regret the lovemaking they'd shared, even though she knew that her final memories of him would be of an angry, thwarted man...but even that wouldn't kill her love.

Danielle sighed. As tired as she was of the lies and half-truths, she couldn't come clean with Rico. If she did, she'd lose him forever. And she wasn't ready to face the pain of that moment yet. But she wasn't going to lie, even by omission, to her father for another day.

Towelling her face dry, she muttered impatiently when she realised that she'd left her purse at the table. She didn't even have a smudge of fresh lipstick to hide behind. A quick glance in the mirror revealed a paler-than-normal face and wide eyes that looked peculiarly childlike for a woman who'd just discovered herself in love. No evidence existed of the lovestruck signs that might give her away.

Closing the bathroom door behind her, the sound of raised voices caused her to quicken her pace until she was running down the passage.

"Don't think you can use my daughter to further your own ambitions, D'Alessio," her father roared so loudly that she could hear him through the heavy door.

"Whatever happened to calling me Rico?"

Danielle shut her eyes at the humour in her husband's voice. She could imagine his dark face, his lip curved in amusement. It would drive her father mad.

"You're dealing with me now, not a starry-eyed female."

"Shut up, Sinclair." Rico sounded savage, all traces of humour had vanished. "You have no idea what you're talking about."

Danielle heard the scuffle of feet and knew she dared not lurk out here for much longer. The vision of the two men coming to blows made her twist the heavy brass door handle.

"I'm warning you." Her father's voice rose. "I'll cut her off without a cent—"

She pushed the door open and took in the way the men stood nose-to-nose. "Daddy, what's going on here? Rico's a guest in your house and he's my husband."

"I'll see to it that you never work…" Her father's voice trailed off as her words registered. He turned. "Hardly a husband, Danielle," he said dismissively.

Her chin went up a notch as she met her father's gaze. "You're wrong. Rico is my legal husband."

"Danielle—" She stilled Rico with a raised finger and shot him a glance imploring him to let her speak. He closed his eyes and lowered himself into a chair.

"We're legally married, Daddy."

Her words finally penetrated. She saw the shock in her father's eyes. "Legally married? When did this happen?"

"The day after the church ceremony."

"Are you stupid, girl?" His face turned a dark red, and his voice rose. "I was just warning him about trying something like this."

Out of the corner of her eye she saw a flash of movement as Rico rose to his feet.

"Watch how you talk to my wife. You'll address her with respect," he growled, his gaze relentless.

Her father's eyes grew fearful. *He's scared of Rico.* Satisfaction curled through her.

"Apologise!" Rico loomed over the shorter man, looking deadly. "You can say what you like to me. But take care of how you talk to Danielle."

Her father had clearly decided Rico looked like a man

who'd reached the end of his tether. He sidled away and sank into a chair. "Sorry, Danielle." The apology sounded forced. "Your announcement surprised me."

She suppressed a smile at the reluctant concession. "Daddy, you don't need to worry about Rico being after my trust fund, he's got enough millions of his own."

"Millions?" He threw Rico a furious look. "He's been working in the Third World. Don't be taken in," her father sneered.

"I can vouch that he's got more than a cent to his name. He's been insisting on purchasing large items for the townhouse."

"He trying to impress you."

Danielle laughed. "I can't believe that you don't know how successful his kidnap retrieval operation has been. Pascal even said he'd read about it. And that's without the fortune—"

"Fortune?" Robert Sinclair barked, turning on Rico. "Is this a scam? Or have you been gun running? How else would you get your hands on millions?"

"Aside from the millions I made legitimately, I inherited several more from my late wife. You may have heard of the family. Ravaldi." Rico's mouth slanted. "Alessandro Ravaldi. Perhaps that name rings a bell."

Danielle began to pay attention. Even she had heard of the Italian gazillionaire.

"Who hasn't heard of Ravaldi," her father dismissed.

"Alessandro is my late wife's brother."

"My God." Robert Sinclair gazed at Rico with grudging respect. "That must make you—"

"Rich. Yes." Rico smiled. But it wasn't a comfortable smile, and Danielle watched her father, waiting for him to back down at the realisation that Rico could afford everything he owned.

But her father didn't give an inch. "So what's in this marriage for you?" he challenged.

A silence fell over the room. Danielle counted the beats off the second hand of the elegant antique grandfather clock in the corner, until she could bear it no longer. "Daddy, don't—"

"You're still after my daughter." Her father turned to glare at her. "And I'm damned if I'm letting him get his hands on you." His expression changed, and Danielle didn't like the contempt that she saw in her father's eyes. "That's what this elaborate farce is all about, isn't it? Despite your protestations of innocence all those years ago."

Did her father know what she'd done all those years ago? Going to Rico's room, trying to seduce him. God, she hoped not! Suddenly Danielle wished the silence was back. "Rico was *innocent*. He didn't do anything four years ago."

"I don't believe that. You were besotted with him. And am I supposed to believe it was all innocent between him and Kim, too?"

Her father did know! "He did nothing. I misinterpreted the sympathy he offered after Mother's death and threw myself at him. He never wanted any part of what I offered, and Kim admitted that he didn't do anything. She changed her statement."

"Hmm…I wonder. Pity, that she didn't see fit to attend tonight."

"Frankly, I'm not surprised—she's ashamed! She made a play for a married man who turned her down. Flat."

"So I'm supposed to believe you rejected both my daughters four years ago." Robert Sinclair stared at Rico for a long moment. "So what are you getting out of this marriage deal, D'Alessio?

Rico stared at her father. "What does one usually get from marriage?"

"Money? Children?"

"Well, the first doesn't matter to me, but an heir wouldn't come amiss."

"An heir?" Her father's gaze widened, and he shot a look of disbelief at Danielle.

Her knees started to shake as she waited for the axe to fall. Instead her father started to laugh. Clenching her fists against her ears, she cried, "Stop it, Daddy! Or I'll leave."

Before her father could say a word, Rico's arm came to rest under her elbow. "What a good idea. I think it's time for us to go."

Danielle sagged against Rico, trembling with relief as he escorted her out of the house after a terse farewell, leaving her father alone at the elaborate doorway to stare after them.

"Don't let your father bother you."

The bedroom was bathed in soft light, the curtains drawn and Rico lay under the covers of the big bed beside her.

"I won't," Danielle said slowly. "He's never going to change. I've finally accepted that. I have to, or I'll have no choice but to walk away from him altogether—and I don't want to do that."

Pushing the heavy covers aside, Danielle rested her head against his broad bare chest. The slow, solid beat of Rico's heart beneath her ear was oddly comforting. "But tonight showed me he doesn't have a great deal of respect for me. Perhaps the time has come for me to leave the security that the Sinco umbrella has always offered. Try my wings out, fly a little."

"I respect you, Danielle D'Alessio." Rico placed a soft kiss against her hair. "You're a hell of a woman, do you know that?"

Something inside her melted. She turned into his arms, breast to chest, and rested her chin on his breastbone. "Thank you."

Her eyes met his and they shared an instant of complete

understanding that made Danielle feel as though she'd accomplished an overwhelming feat, a bit like the flying she'd talked about.

"Whatever you try, you'll be a success. I'll remind you of that one day." Rico gave her a slow smile.

But even his smile couldn't stop the cold wash of dread from running over her. The warm contentment she'd felt drained away as she said, "But you won't be here. I need to learn to find my way alone." She felt Rico recoil. Quickly she murmured, "Rico?"

"Does that mean you no longer need me in your bed, either? That you'll satisfy your newly discovered desires alone?"

"No!" She stared at him, regret searing her. "I wasn't talking about right now. I was musing aloud about the future."

"Of course! The future. I'll have my son or daughter...and you'll have some executive position in some important company."

Pain shattered inside her, icy splinters piercing her heart, until she wanted to shout out loud that that wasn't what she wanted. She loved him, dammit! So why the hell couldn't he love her back?

But he was already rolling over, taking her with him, trapping her beneath the hard bulk of his body. "Enough talk, let's get down to action."

The angry note in his voice made her wriggle beneath him in an effort to escape, reluctant to make love like this. "Rico, maybe not—"

"—tonight, because I've got a headache, hmm?" But he lifted his torso so that she could free herself. Thwarted, she lay still and stared up into angry, mocking eyes. Suddenly she wanted to wipe that masculine fury clean off his face.

"Where's the respect you promised me only minutes ago?" she retorted, holding him at bay with palms pressed against his chest. "I demand respect from the man who shares my bed, understand?" Danielle raised an eyebrow and watched his mouth drop open.

She gave him a shove, and he rolled back against the pillows. Danielle pushed the covers away from his body and quickly twisted around until she was kneeling on the bed beside him. "Do you understand?" With tantalisingly slow movements she began to unbutton the row of tiny buttons down the front of her nightdress.

He swallowed. "Yes, Princess. I understand…perfectly."

"Good," she purred, and lifted a slim leg over his hips. Lowering herself, she straddled him. His body jerked beneath her, and she rewarded him with a slow smile. Heat penetrated every nerve ending, banishing the empty ache his mockery had created. Arousal flamed through her, and she felt him harden beneath her thighs. The passion promised to knock the pain out her mind, to replace it with a hot need that she could embrace and share with Rico, until satisfaction claimed them both, granting an escape from obstacles that seemed insurmountable.

Filled with bravado by his response, she bent over him, caught his wrist and directed his hands to the wooden slats of the headboard. "Now hold on, I don't want to lose you during the ride," she said, shooting him a sultry smile.

"Oh, my hell!" Rico's eyes were wide with a combination of shock and surprise.

A heady confidence that she'd never known swelled inside her at the sight of the awe on Rico's face. The hem of the night-gown was soft under her fingers and she lifted it, swishing it from side to side as it rose higher, exposing tantalising glimpses of her tummy…then tugged again. Aside from Rico's rough breathing, the only sound in the room was the whisper of silk against skin.

For a moment she wondered what she was doing, whether

she could carry this impromptu seduction off. A chill of uncertainty swept her as memory flashed of another time she'd stripped off in front of him. And his harsh rejection. But this time it was different. She was a woman now—not an insecure girl. And this time Rico was free to love her. Now was no time to get cold feet. Especially not under the heat of his heavy-lidded gaze. Taking a deep breath, Danielle threw caution to the winds and whipped the nightie over her head.

The expression on Rico's face as he gazed at her naked body told her that she was doing something right. She sat back, hooked her hands into the waistband of the boxers he wore and slid them down his thighs. Rico assisted by kicking them off. She rewarded him with another of those slow smiles that made his eyes go darker than the bitterest chocolate.

Then she leaned forward and brushed her breasts against his chest, the scattering of dark hair creating a friction that made her nipples tighten and caused a rush of tingles. Simultaneously she moved her lower body against his in slow sweeps.

Rico raised his hips in an insistent rhythm, and uttered a throaty groan. His hand came around the back of her neck and pulled her lips down to his. His mouth was hot and hungry. At her eager response, his mouth grew more demanding, his body vibrating beneath hers.

"Didn't I tell you to hold on to the headboard?" she murmured in his ear, then bit his earlobe.

"Witch!" The hand against her nape tightened. "I couldn't keep my hands off you," he growled. And matched his actions to his words by running his other hand across her shoulder, along the indent of her spine, to rest at the base of her spine and draw her closer. At the unremitting pressure her heart hammered, and she shifted until she felt him—there at the entrance to her core.

She nudged him, but instead of the penetration she craved, he moved against her, his hardness filling the hidden furrow. Slowly he slid to and fro, until she wanted to scream as the heat built relentlessly inside her.

"Ngh…" She tried to thrash her head from side to side, but he held her tightly, sealing her mouth with his. Wildly she licked the inside of his lower lip, and immediately he increased the pace of the rocking against her. She shuddered, grimacing, then her skin pulled tight around her body.

She moaned, her body tensing.

Swiftly he rolled over, holding her against him, under him, and, pressing his face into the junction between her jaw and her shoulder, he plunged into her frenzied body, driven beyond the boundaries of his control.

Danielle cried out, a hoarse sound that made him instantly respond by tonguing the tender skin beneath her ear. Shivers raced across her skin, and the contractions rippled through her until her whole body quivered in reaction. He groaned, the speed of his thrusts increased, and then he started to shudder.

After a long silence her murmured, "Danielle," his arms tightening around her. Then, "You're something else, *cara*. Wow!"

Her breath caught at the note in his voice. Wordlessly she snuggled closer. It took a while for her to come down from the high that their intense lovemaking had created. As she lay in Rico's arms and stared into the dark while his chest rose and fell evenly beneath her ear, Danielle struggled to sleep. Discovering that she loved him had changed everything.

Because love went hand in hand with trust.

And she'd lied to Rico, deceived him.

Her heart fluttered with anxiety. There was no doubt that once she revealed the extent of her deception she'd lose him. Rico wouldn't stay.

Not for a woman like her.

# Ten

*"Danielle!"*

His head pounding, Rico burst through the glass sliding doors onto the patio, his gaze frantically searching for Danielle. Three long paces took him to where she crouched over an arrangement of ceramic pots.

"What the *hell* are you doing!"

"Planting pots."

She was staring at him as if he'd taken leave of his senses. *Perhaps he had.* He raked a shaking hand through his hair and inhaled deeply to slow the adrenaline that had rushed through him when he'd entered the house and failed instantly to locate her.

He'd left her in the sitting room to answer the doorbell. It had been Ken Pascal, Sinco's head of security. Rico had gone with Ken to collect a dossier from the other man's car. He hadn't wanted Danielle standing in the street. Leaving her safely inside had seemed the lesser of two evils. Except had she stayed put? No.

He glared at her down-bent head. Her bare hands were plunged deep into a mix of rich, dark soil. "You should be wearing gloves."

Danielle squinted back up at him. "I like the feel of potting soil beneath my hands. It's therapeutic." She picked up a punnet of seedlings and deftly pushed the small green plants into the hollows she'd created.

"What are those?" he asked, as his heart rate slowly returned to normal.

"Impatiens. People often call them busy lizzies."

"Oh." The silence stretched reminding him of how withdrawn she'd been all day. Moodiness was the last thing he'd expected after the wild sex they'd shared last night. Maybe she was coming down with something. He pointed to another plastic holder filled with fine-leafed plants. "And those?"

"Lobelia," she replied.

"Where are you going to plant them?"

"I thought I'd use them as a border, plant them around the edge of the pot and let them trail over the side."

"You enjoy this, don't you?"

"You mean getting my hands dirty?" She glanced up. "I love it. Gardening in the evenings after a day at the office is always a good time for me to work out my frustrations—and to think."

Rico wasn't sure if he liked the sound of that. "What do you need to think about today?"

Her gaze fell, shrouding her eyes from his scrutiny. "Oh, this and that."

"Be more specific," he suggested, tension winding tight inside him.

"I was thinking about what I said last night, about moving on from Sinco." But she kept her head bowed, and Rico had a frustrated notion that she'd been thinking about more than her career path. The idea that she was hiding stuff from him drove him wild. He hunkered down beside her. "So what happens next?"

"I'll place the pots in a shady position and water them each day. Watch them grow. Soon the flowers will burst into colour."

That wasn't what he'd meant, but he didn't have the heart to bring her back to a topic she clearly didn't want to discuss. He let it rest. "And when they've finished flowering, what then?"

"Impatiens often self-seed themselves. They'll grow thicker next year. Very efficient plants, they know how to create the next generation." Her tone was strange, almost flat, but she was smiling at him.

Rico dismissed his unease. "I thought we might go out for a meal, you need a break." Early this morning Danielle had called Martin Dunstan and unearthed the day care proposal her father had mentioned last night. She'd worked on it all day like a woman possessed. Was her father responsible for her gloominess? Awkwardly he placed an arm around her shoulder. She stiffened. Damn. When he made love to her, he could touch her confidently enough, so why did he feel so inept now? Flattening his hand, he slid it down her back, then up again.

"Where do you want to go?"

She turned to face him, and his hand fell away. Her eyes glistened with emotion like a silvery cloak of dew on a lawn at daybreak. "Could we have dinner at home? Just you and me?"

His chest contracted. "Of course. If that's what you want."

"Rico, why do you have to be so damn nice sometimes?" Her voice was husky.

"Hey." He placed a finger under her chin and tilted it up. "Am I such an ogre to live with?"

The glimmer in her eyes grew brighter. "Never an ogre."

"Only a dinosaur?" he teased gently.

She launched herself across the space that separated them. "Oh, Rico!" She threw her arms around his neck and locked them tight, until he could hardly breathe.

"Hey." Falling to his knees, he closed his arms around her, inhaling her warm, flowery scent. The smell of soil and the plants was sharp and unfamiliar to him, but it was a perfume he could get used to. Bending his head over hers, he started to plan an evening of quiet relaxation…although snatches of more sensual images he hurriedly suppressed kept interrupting.

"Dinner at home it is."


While Rico grilled snapper, Danielle tossed a salad together. She cut fat wedges of lemon to accompany the succulent fish. During dinner she tried her best to behave normally, but Rico's sharp glances revealed that she hadn't been wholly successful. Deception did not sit well with her and she was growing increasingly uncomfortable with the extent that she had deceived Rico. She suspected she wouldn't find any peace until she told him exactly what was troubling her. Of course, her peace of mind would bear a price—the loss of Rico.

After the meal Danielle dropped onto the couch and picked up a copy of *NZ House & Garden,* but she barely saw the brightly coloured photos of the family homes as she paged listlessly through. All she could see was Rico, kneeling in front of her pots, his expression soft…almost caring…after he'd teased her.

"Coffee?" asked Rico.

Danielle set the magazine aside and wrinkled her nose. "I seem to have lost the taste for it. I might have a cup of hot chocolate later."

When Rico joined her on the couch, the cloying aroma of his espresso coffee coupled with the edgy restlessness that filled her made her feel slightly ill. Picking up a cushion, she tucked it in behind her back. "Rico, we have to talk."

"That sounds ominous," he commented, setting his coffee mug down.

Her small smile did little to ease her misery. "I think perhaps the time has come for us to be honest with each other."

His expression grew wary. "Honest? I've always told you the truth." He scanned her face. "But perhaps you have things you've been hiding, hmm? Spit them out, they can't be so bad that we can't work them out."

He'd find out soon enough that they were worse than he could imagine. But for now she clung to the first part of his statement. "I think there are things that you haven't told me. Last night it became clear to me that my father seems to think that you—" she searched for the right words "—tried something with me four years ago. I didn't think he knew about that night."

Rico said nothing, but his eyes narrowed to dark cracks.

Both she and Kim had caused Rico harm. Danielle shuddered. "You should never have left." The words *run away* hung in the air between them. "You should have stood trial if you were charged."

He gave her a look that burned with bitterness. "I know that. But I had no choice."

"Because my father told Lucia that you'd go to prison for what Kim said had happened? You could have fought that, proved your innocence."

"I shouldn't have needed to." It burst from him. "A man is presumed innocent until proven guilty. Except when Robert Sinclair is involved…then the onus changes. I was fighting a battle I could never win, given the manufactured evidence."

"What do you mean?"

"Those damn white lacy panties."

Perplexed, Danielle frowned at him. "What?"

"The panties," he uttered impatiently. "I suppose you must've wondered where they appeared from."

She had? She knew nothing about any lace panties. Danielle waited for him to continue.

"The night before the fracas with Kimberly, you came to my room, remember?"

How could she ever forget? The old humiliation scorched her, and she huddled into a ball in the furthest corner of the couch.

"You took that white robe off and underneath you were wearing nothing but a pair of white, floral lace panties."

Shamed, wanting to forget his fury and outrage, Danielle closed her eyes. She'd had a huge crush on him. She could see herself that night, running barefoot down the corridor back to her suite, her hair streaming behind her, her robe flapping, hastily pulled on, as she sought the sanctuary of her bedroom. She'd wanted nothing more than a quiet place to lick the wound that Rico's uncompromising rejection had opened. Instead she'd run full tilt into Kim, who'd caught her arm and demanded to know where she'd been. She'd refused to say a word.

In her room she'd flung herself onto her bed, tears streaming down her face, while Kim had perched on the bed edge. It had been a tempest of weeping, full of the pent-up misery from her mother's death, the crashing realisation that Rico did not share what she felt about him. The next day events had started to snowball until she felt as if her heart was splintering.

But she hadn't left her briefs behind, she'd still been wearing them. The same lacy style she still wore. Boring perhaps. But she liked the comfort of the familiar. "Your memory is good—I don't remember the panties."

Rico gave her a strange look. "I never forgot them, seeing that they were a key component in the investigation against me."

Her gaze shot to his face. "What do you mean?"

"When I came out of the shower to find Kimberly in my bed the following night, she was wearing even less. She whipped back the covers to surprise me with her nakedness."

*Oh, God.*

"I threw her out, tossing her nightdress after her. But she left a souvenir in the bottom of my bed."

Danielle thought furiously. "Panties?"

"You got it. Your white lace panties."

She froze. "Mine?" *Kim.* Her sister couldn't have been so cruel. Had she really intended Danielle's panties to be found in Rico's bed?

He nodded. "Yep. The police found them. Apparently Kim didn't own white panties. Plus there were forensic traces of your presence—a long blonde hair—in my room from the previous night. Which was why your father thought you and I were…involved."

She gasped. "So Daddy thought I was sleeping with you?" The irony of it! Rico had rejected both her and Kim—in two nights. Her father couldn't have left his two teenaged daughters in safer care.

"Your father pointed out that when his turn in the witness box came he would have to identify the garment as yours, to do otherwise would be to commit perjury. He told me that you had reacted to the prospect by threatening to commit suicide because you couldn't face the scandal that would erupt."

"That's a lie! I never even knew about those damn panties." *Oh, Kim!*

Rico's breath caught, the sound loud in the room. "The lying bastard! I believed him. I thought you must know what Kim had done. Your father demanded that I leave the country, return my Sinco shares to him, in return he'd have the investigation quashed. He said he'd pay what he needed to 'make it go away,' that Kim—and particularly you—didn't need the notoriety that would result if I stayed."

"Oh, dear God!"

"You'd been through a tough time. Your mother had died. For months I'd watched you bottle up the grief without having an outlet. You had a crush on me. I tried to be gentle with you—you so desperately needed counselling. I wasn't surprised that you'd snapped. I thought my…rejection…had been the final nail in the coffin."

Oh, heck. He'd felt guilty. She—and her family—had royally screwed up his life.

"There'd been so much lost already. Lucia was hysterical. Your father did a good job on her. My marriage was over—even my wife had tried and convicted me. But we had a child to think about and I refused to be beholden to my wife's family. My life had fallen apart," Rico continued. "I didn't want *your* death on my conscience, too. It was enough that your mother's death kept me awake. It seemed easier to go than to fight about my innocence."

Her father had manipulated him—and Lucia. She said, "Your wife was silly, she should've trusted you."

His head snapped back. Danielle waited for his anger to erupt in his dead wife's defence. Instead he said, "Lucia was…possessive."

"But what about the baby? You should've defended yourself for your child's sake."

"I tried. She didn't believe me." Rico raked his hands through his hair. "As if I'd look at another woman when I had

Lucia—and a teenager at that. But she was a passionate woman." He gave a tiny smile. "She was, after all, Italian."

His words caused a pang inside her. He'd loved his wife. "But to kill herself…" How could she have deserted Rico in such a cruel way?

"I blame myself."

"No!" Danielle reached out to him, then dropped her hand. It lay on the sofa between them. "You mustn't. You did not cause her death." If anyone was to blame, it was her father. The realisation caused her chest to constrict. No wonder Rico hated the Sinclairs. No wonder he wanted revenge. But his revenge wasn't possible. And she had to break it to him. That she'd misled him…lied to him…for her own ends.

"There's a horrible irony in the fact that you thought I was at risk of killing myself, then your wife killing herself."

"Don't I know it."

His despair deepened her urge to throw her arms around him, but it was overridden by the corrosive knowledge that she first had to tell him her secret. So she hugged her arms tightly around her own ribs instead and considered how he'd feel once he discovered that the teenager he'd gone into exile for rather than see die, had become a woman who'd lied to him….

At the strident call of the telephone she leaped up, only to realise that it was Rico's cell phone that summoned. She collapsed back onto the couch, vaguely surprised by the rising and falling cadences of Rico's voice speaking in Italian. She blanked it out, more concerned about how to tell him that she could never have the baby that he so desperately wanted.

A muted click announced that the call was over. Danielle raised her eyes, stilling as she saw the dark turmoil in his.

"I have to go to Italy."

"What? *Now?*"

He nodded, his face suddenly haggard and pale against his

dark hair. "I'll leave as soon as I can get a flight. My father is in hospital and he's asking for me."

Danielle barely heard him making reservations. His father was ill? She hadn't even known. What else was he still keeping from her? Would he never share himself with her? But then why should he? She didn't deserve his trust.

Danielle waited for him to finish booking his flight. Then she said, "I'm so sorry. What's the matter with your father?"

Rico walked toward her, frowning. "He had a stroke three months ago. It turned out to be minor. He isn't feeling well, so they've taken him back to hospital. He's asking for me. I need to be there."

He was worried that his father might die, she realised as she glimpsed the pain and uncertainty in his eyes.

"Danielle...I don't want to leave you. Come with me. I mentioned that I'd gotten married. My family would love to meet you."

"No!" He needed the time with his family; she'd be little more than an impostor. "Not at this time. Your family needs you...I'll be fine."

He hesitated, his eyes dark. "I'll get Ken to arrange a body-guard for you, extra security—and a driver."

Something about his statement tugged at her mind, some-thing she knew she should tell him. She tried to focus on it, but the fragment of thought vanished.

Already she could sense his distraction. But then, just as she thought she'd lost him, Rico bent towards her, his gaze intent. "I don't like the idea of leaving."

"It doesn't matter, Rico, honestly." Then she shivered as the last word struck home.

"Are you sure?"

She nodded. "I'm sure," she croaked, her throat aching.

"Okay, next time you'll come with me. Perhaps when our

baby is born, to show my parents." A slight smile accompa-
nied his words and there was a gleam of hope in his eyes.

*Our baby.*

Danielle's heart stopped and her blood iced in her chest.
Unexpectedly the moment of truth had reared up in front of
her, and she knew she could no longer ignore it. A calm descended upon her, the kind that cleared her mind and numbed
her insides. Taking a deep breath, she said quietly, "Rico,
there won't be a baby."

He froze. "What the devil do you mean? You can't call it
off, not now. I've just told my family we're married for God's
sake."

"I'm not going to call it off. You are. Or at least you will,
once you understand what I'm trying to say." Cold enfolded
her. She shivered. With great deliberation, so that there would
be no chance of a misunderstanding, she said, "Rico, I can't
have children. I'm sterile. Because of the accident."

She heard his breath catch. Her hands clenched and she
barely felt the pain of her nails biting into her palm. Knowing
that she was deluding herself, she waited for him to say that
it didn't matter, that all he wanted was *her.*

His face revealed no emotion. "My father wants nothing
more than a grandson. I'm the last male to carry the D'Alessio
name."

*The last of the line.* Danielle shut her eyes. So it was over.
This was as much an obstacle as his need for revenge. And this
time there was no way out, no compromise that they could
reach. And why should he compromise? It wasn't as if he loved
her.

Her heart heavy as lead, she stared at the ceiling. In the corner
a crack had appeared in the paintwork beside the cornice. She'd
have all the time in the world to fix it, paint the whole damn house
if necessary. At least it would keep her busy after he'd gone.

"Did you plan this?" he asked with icy ferocity.

"What?" she asked, playing for time.

"Did you plan this—your revenge?"

*Dear God.* "Revenge was *your* plan. Remember?"

"So you didn't see this as an opportunity to thwart me?"

She hesitated. And then it was too late.

"So that's it." His tone was hard edged. "Funny thing is I was starting to feel I'd been too hard on you, that I was in danger of destroying your gentleness in my quest for revenge. Well, all round, you get last laugh."

She'd never felt less like laughing in her life. Any victory she'd anticipated on that day when he'd threatened to smash Kim's marriage if she didn't marry him and provide him with a child, was hollow.

Quietly, in an effort to salvage something between them, she said, "Rico, I lost the ability to have a child. You lost an unborn baby. We're kind of at the same place and—"

"Don't try to make out we have anything in common. You have *absolutely* no idea of how I feel at this moment." The flat note of finality in his tone was as audible as the click of a door locking.

There was no point in trying to sway him. He would never understand how she'd felt on learning that she'd never bear children. Or the agony when she'd realised that she could no longer bear the notion of training to be a kindergarten teacher, surrounded all day by the children. Her future had been irrevocably sealed off by a cruel act of fate. What man could ever want her?

She would have plenty of time to cry later. Now the important thing was to get out of this…disaster…with as much dignity as possible.

"No, I don't know how you feel right now. Nor will I ever be able to imagine the hell you must have gone through after

Lucia's death. I'll arrange an appointment with a solicitor to start divorce proceedings." But she couldn't prevent herself from saying, a trifle bitterly, "Then you won't have to worry about further ties to any of the Sinclairs who have caused you nothing but grief."

Her outburst was met with total silence.

At last he said, "I must go or I'll miss my flight."

And softly, her heart breaking, she whispered, "Goodbye, Rico." But he didn't hear—or maybe he just didn't care.

# Eleven

"Goddammit!" In the first-class lounge of Los Angles International Airport, Rico downed another scotch, ignoring the warnings of jetlag.

He felt as if a part of him had been torn out. Hollow. When had she crept under his skin? The anger inside him escalated at the notion. *Why did he even care?*

She'd lied to him. Deliberately deceived him!

He was better off without her.

But railing against Danielle was not improving his mood. He felt betrayed and angry and heartsore. For a long time he sat, his head bent, his hands hanging between his knees, until he could think *without* the world turning red.

Calm at last, he started to mull over his conversation with Danielle. He didn't want a divorce. He knew with certainty that he couldn't leave things…unfinished between them. He was not letting her go. She was not going to walk away from him with that sexy, provocative swing of her hips. Suddenly he didn't care whether she could bear babies or not. He only knew that Danielle had made him laugh when he had no longer cared about living or dying.

She had shown him a path to a future where he was no longer an automaton, to a place bright with hope and the sound of laughter, a place lacking the dark, endless despair that had haunted him for years and driven him to reckless disregard for his own safety.

*Call her!* He pulled his cell phone out his pocket, then he hesitated, not sure what exactly he was prepared to offer. A temporary relationship based on passion? Or something more…enduring? Could he forgive her lie, her terrible deception? Or was he only prepared to indulge the physical attraction that flared between them. How long would it take before the heat burned out? A month? A year? And where would that leave his father's wish to hold his grandson?

So many questions…so many decisions to make. What was he to tell his family? That his bride was infertile? Or that he wasn't ready for fatherhood yet? Confusion raged inside him, until he could no longer think straight. But one thing was clear—before he could return to Danielle, he needed to come to terms with the past.

Slowly he pressed the keypad of his cell phone, calling up the contact list. He had ghosts of his own to lay to rest. An efficient receptionist answered on the first ring. Taking a deep breath, he said, "Alessandro Ravaldi, please."

The bodyguard, whom Rico had apparently briefed last night from the airport, leaned against the counter, sipping the last of his coffee. Tymon, not Tyson—Danielle still kept forgetting his name—was silent and respectful. Under normal circumstances his tall, well-built body would've given her reason for a second glance. But he wasn't Rico.

Tymon's cell phone rang. "The driver's here."

"Who is it?" she asked urgently.

"Bob Harvey."

Her heart sank. *That* was what she'd wanted to tell Rico—about the uncomfortable feeling the man gave her. Too late now. But as soon as she got to the office she'd contact Ken Pascal. She picked up her briefcase and walked to wait by the door while Tymon checked that the way out was clear. When the horn sounded, she pulled the front door shut and shot across the pavement into the waiting car, and Tymon climbed in behind her.

The ride to the office took forever and she couldn't help thinking about how strange it would be not to share an office with Rico. She would have to get used to the feeling, because it was going to last a very long time.

But she had other things to think about—confronting her father, for one.


A shove sent the office door flying back, and Danielle strode determinedly into her father's domain on the tenth floor. Robert Sinclair half rose from his chair, but on seeing who'd created the disturbance he sank back. "You should've had yourself announced. Far more professional, Danielle."

"Why did you tell Rico I'd threatened to kill myself?"

His gaze flickered. "What are you talking about?"

"Don't lie to me! He told me. Did you think he wouldn't?"

For a moment she thought her father might try bluff his way out. Then he shrugged. "Is this important?"

"Yes! Rico left the country, went to work in terrible places, because you lied to him. Was it because you wanted his Sinco shares?"

"He was a fool to believe me. I never thought he'd accept it so easily—or that he'd be swayed by it."

"Rico is a man of deep feelings." And her family had done nothing but cheat and lie to him. Dark despair closed in on her. *How could he ever love her?*

Her father had resumed reading the financial pages strewn across his desk, and anger surged through her, its strength overcoming her despair. "You told him that you would testify to the world that the undergarment found in Rico's bed was mine, and you said that when you'd explained to me what you intended to do, I vowed to commit suicide."

Robert Sinclair lifted his shoulders carelessly. "He was guilty. He deserved to go to prison."

Contempt cooled her anger. "It was never Kim. It was *you* who planted that pair of panties in his bed."

He shrugged. "It had been reported that you'd been seen visiting his room the night before. Who did D'Alessio think he was? Messing with my daughters?"

*Poor Rico.* Danielle stared at her father. Then said very softly, "Thank God Rico isn't like you."

Her father set his jaw. "Now look here—"

"No, you listen to me and get this straight because it's the last time I'm ever going to say it. Four years ago Rico never laid a finger on me—as much as I wanted him to. The man respected his marriage vows, and I was too much of an airhead to realise what kind of predicament I placed him in."

"D'Alessio shouldn't have gone if he never touched Kim, he should've taken his chances with the jury."

"Kim lied. And you put him in a horrible position. You terrified his wife, told him that I might commit suicide. The man was innocent, and after his wife died, he was past caring." Danielle gave a snort of disgust. "Were you ever unfaithful to Mother?"

"No!" Shock drove the colour out of his face leaving it pale. "Never! I loved your mother."

"Do you think she'd approve of the way you've behaved to Rico?"

His lips drained of colour, but he said nothing.

"Mother *liked* Rico. And do you want to hear something ironic?" She gave a bitter little laugh. "Rico is eaten up with guilt because Mother died. He seems to believe he could've single-handedly prevented it."

"That's ridiculous. I asked him to escort you and your mother to that concert. I planned to bring Kim and meet you there and let Rico take my car home. How could he have been responsible for an accident that happened on the way?"

"He feels partially to blame because they switched seats. Mother wanted to sit up front, where Rico was going to sit. He believes *he* should've died. That's why he was so kind to me after the accident, because I was wild with grief and struggling to cope on my own, because he felt responsible for the pain I'd suffered. I repaid his compassion with infatuation." She glared at her father. "And you rewarded him by destroying his life."

Her father looked shattered. "I never realised that you were so…affected. You always appeared so calm, so controlled. I thought your youth had cushioned you from the full weight of grief, that—"

Disbelief warred with fury. "I was trapped in a car for hours with my mother. I heard her groaning, and then she died, damn it."

"Rose was alive?"

"I *heard* her dying. And I was so helpless. All I had was Rico. He stayed beside me and never let go of my hand through those terrible hours."

Her father came around the desk in a rush. "I never knew."

He sounded broken. "I thought…perhaps I closed my mind to it because I wanted to believe…that she died on impact." Hesitantly he said, "I've failed you, haven't I? And I've failed Rose."

It was awful to watch him crumple as his head dropped into his hands. "I found it so difficult to come to terms with your mother's death, to survive without her. I'd assumed she'd always be there. That one day, after I'd achieved what I set out to, she'd be there waiting for me. And then one summer day my dream was gone." He raised his head, his eyes desolate. "I didn't know what to do—how I was going to get through the empty days."

Slowly all the hurt drained out of her. Danielle swallowed, and found that the lump in her throat made it difficult. Tears welled in her eyes as she softly said, "I thought work was all you cared about."

"You were too young for me to talk to."

"Mum's death matured me." A half step brought her closer to her father. "I still miss her."

His eyes glittered with moisture. "So do I…so do I." And he opened his arms.

"Where is your wife?"

Umberto D'Alessio's voice was loud in the private room. Rico's mother, Bianca, sat in a chair beside the hospital bed, holding a hand that she kept stroking, while Bella poured him a glass of juice.

Rico noted that in the space of a day his father already looked much better. "She's in New Zealand. We both agreed that I should get to your side as quickly as possible."

"But I am not dying. You should've brought her. I want to see this woman who will bear your children." With a sly glance in Rico's direction, he added, "Why only today the specialist was saying that I'm in very good shape for a man of seventy.

Maybe I will come out to New Zealand and see this wife myself?"

"Perhaps we wait awhile, Umberto," Rico's mother suggested tactfully.

A remarkable recovery. Rico narrowed his eyes for an instant. Then shook his head. No, Umberto *had* suffered a stroke. That hadn't been faked. But perhaps he'd exaggerated the severity?

His father sat up, demanding that Bella rearrange the cushions. Rico stepped forward to help raise the back of the hospital bed. When everything was settled to his father's liking, he said, "You're an old rapscallion."

The guilty glance that Umberto shot him proved that his suspicions weren't wholly unfounded. Umberto said quickly, "The news you bring makes me feel better already. You should get back to your new wife. Tell her the family demands to see her." A grin lit up Umberto's weathered face. "What is the lucky woman's name?"

"Danielle."

"Ah, Daniella—a good name, a good choice, my son."

"Danielle, not Daniella, Papa. It suits her."

"Ah, well. And her family name?"

With reluctance Rico added, "Sinclair."

His sister gasped. Umberto's eyes turned black. "Sinclair? This is the name of the family that—"

His mother placed a restraining hand on Umberto's. "Hush, you don't let Rico talk."

"*Si.*" Rico stood straight, determined not to let his tension show. "She's the sister of the girl who accused me."

Suddenly Umberto didn't look so joyous. "Do you not make a mistake, my son?"

Hell, yes. He'd done nothing but make one mistake after the other.

He gave a small smile. "You'll have to decide for yourselves."

"I want to meet her," Bella chimed in. "Any woman who married you, big brother, must have special qualities." The concern on his father's face started to ease.

"I'll tell Danielle she has been summoned," Rico said, even more determined now to stop Danielle's plans for a divorce.

*"Grazie."* His father sounded supremely satisfied, and Rico shot him another sharp look.

"Why do I get the feeling that the old man has been waiting for this day?" he murmured to his sister.

"Maybe because I'm proving too slow to find a husband and Claudia is already married off. Of course, Claudia only has a daughter and that doesn't count," she replied *sotto voce*. "You—the last male in the D'Alessio line—were the final hope."

He grimaced. How could he devastate his family with the news that his wife would never bear his children?

"Rico," Umberto called. "You should tell the Ravaldi family of your remarriage. Alessandro will want to extend his felicitations."

Curtly Rico inclined his head. He'd been dreading that visit—he should've got it over with on his previous visit to Milan several months earlier. But seeing his brother-in-law would have opened raw wounds. After all, Alessandro had lost a sister, a sister whose well-being he'd entrusted to Rico.

Rico's hands fisted. That made it twice that women under his care and protection had died. Rose Sinclair and Lucia Ravaldi both gone.

"I've an appointment to see Alessandro," he revealed, hoping that his brother-in-law would not be too outraged by his second marriage. But his family's delight in his newly remarried state had surprised him. Maybe even Alessandro didn't expect him to mourn forever.

A pair of wide grey-green eyes crept into his mind, and the dimple beside the irrepressible smile. *Danielle*. She'd deceived him. Yet she was sweet, kind and wanted nothing more than his happiness. She'd put up with a lot from him, while she'd been recovering from terrifying threats. His wife had guts.

He should grab what was offered to him, take another risk. But what about children—an heir? He stared at his parents' intertwined hands, watched as his father's fingers tightened convulsively around his mother's. Already Danielle made him feel so many things he'd never experienced before. The intense passion that sizzled when their eyes met, the melting warmth when he said something that made her laugh, the sheer pleasure he found simply being with her.

Suddenly—unexpectedly—he missed her desperately.

A car horn hooted outside.

Damn. Her ride had arrived earlier than yesterday. Danielle splashed more water on her face. The evidence of her sleepless night was there for the world to see in her sad, reddened eyes. A dull ache reverberated through her head. She contemplated climbing back into bed, drawing the covers over her head and letting the day pass in a hazy slumber.

But work was waiting for her. She had to forget Rico and submerge herself in her career. Except, the prospect of a Sinco directorship no longer held the same appeal. She would look for another job. Fly a little. At least then she'd no longer be sitting next to the empty office of her tall, dark and dangerous lover.

As the horn sounded again she grabbed her briefcase and rushed through the front door. "I'm sorry, Tymon, I overslept."

A new chauffeur wearing reflective sunglasses stood beside

the open door of the car. Ken Pascal must've accepted her misgivings about Bob Harvey. She suppressed a grin. The new
chauffeur apparently fancied himself as a Hollywood FBI
extra. Dimly she noticed the car was different, too. She dived
into the back, only to find herself alone.

"Tymon?" she asked, panic rising. The wide back seat was
empty. She tried the door. It was locked. Frantically she
thought back, her mind buzzing. How long had it been since
she'd last heard Tymon? At least fifteen minutes. He'd shouted
up the stairs that he'd made her breakfast—not that she'd had
time to eat it—and then there'd been silence. Was he in on this,
too? Or was he hurt? Her mind shied away from the pos-
sibility that he might be dead.

Danielle banged her briefcase against the tinted windows,
but they were solid. The partition that separated her from the
driver was a dark pane that revealed nothing. "Let me out!"

The car speeded up. Breathing deeply, the taste of fear like
cold metal in her mouth, she tried not to let panic debilitate
her. This was what Rico had been waiting for. This bastard had
toyed with her for far too long. Well, she'd had enough. He
wasn't going to get the better of her.


"You've remarried? May I offer congratulations?" Alessandro embraced Rico, and the tension that had coiled through
Rico all day started to ease.

"Thank you." Rico stepped back, relieved to see Alessandro smiling at him, his fierce tawny eyes filled with pleasure.

"You've been a stranger for too long, Rico."

"I should've visited earlier," he acknowledged. His guilt
hadn't allowed it.

"I'll never understand why you didn't accept my offer of
assistance. It would've secured you the best defence lawyers
in the world."

Rico shrugged, unwilling to reveal how reluctant he'd been to sponge off his wife's family, how foolish he'd been to believe Robert Sinclair's bluff. But if it had been true…

The thought of a world without Danielle made him shudder. Then he hadn't known of her inner strength, had only seen her as one of life's victims. "Lucia didn't believe in my innocence in the end, so what was the point in trying to prove it to a roomful of strangers, hmm?"

"Rico," Alessandro's gaze was level, "I'm going to say this only once. You're alive, you have a life ahead of you. *Let Lucia go.* Remember what you shared but don't idealise her."

"I don't want to forget her, Alessandro," Rico said, wishing the pain would go.

"I know. I loved my sister and I miss her, too. But I wasn't blind to her shortcomings. Don't think I don't know that she could be incredibly headstrong."

Rico had to laugh at Alessandro's knowing expression. "Sometimes," he conceded.

"Many times!" Alessandro cast his eyes heavenwards. "And she had more than eating disorders…and bouts of depression…she was always insecure. *Dio mio,* I remember how pathologically jealous she was—terrified that she'd snatched you too young, that one day you'd fall for a younger woman."

Startled, Rico stared at Alessandro. "That's insane."

"It's true. Why do you think she was so furious about the whole debacle? It was her worst nightmare come true. She thought she'd driven you away by her foolish jealousy."

"*I loved her.* I would never've been tempted by another woman," Rico said, angry at the very idea that his loyalty, his honour, was at issue. Although in the deepest corner of his brain a splinter of guilt festered. He hadn't been totally unaware of the eighteen-year old Danielle. How could he forget the anguish that had melded them together while her mother died? And he remembered too damn well how little she'd worn in his room that night, her wide grey-green eyes full of adoration. But he would *never* have betrayed Lucia.

"I know that." Alessandro patted his shoulder. "I never doubted you for an instant. And I told that to Lucia. But she wanted to make you sweat—to suffer." He sighed. "What people do to their loved ones makes me pleased I've never risked matrimony. And here you are, ready for love again."

"I don't l—" Rico bit off the rest of the denial, before he had to face a barrage of questions about exactly why he had married Danielle. Suddenly his reasons didn't seem terribly honourable.

Her clear eyes, the up-tilted chin, the wicked sense of humour, should've warned him that she'd never be a pushover. But had he looked for the signs? No, he'd simply steamrolled her into what he wanted, giving little in return.

Alessandro was right. He had a second chance at happiness. It was time to say goodbye to Lucia.

When his cell phone started its insistent ring, Rico impatiently checked the identity of the caller, about to divert it to voice mail. But when he saw the Auckland number displayed, his heart started to pound. "D'Alessio," he answered curtly.

"Rico!" The use of his first name captured his attention, but it was the stark pain in Robert Sinclair's voice that made his knees go weak. The older man's next words drove all thought out of his head, until all that remained was cold, numbing agony.

"Hey—" a hand shook him "—are you okay?"

Rico wrenched his mind away from the horrors he was imagining and stared into Alessandro's concerned eyes. His mouth felt parched and he swallowed, his chest burning. But he dared not reveal the depth of his pain, in case he never managed to bottle it up again.

Instead he said in a dull, lifeless tone, "My wife has been kidnapped."

# Twelve

"You!" Danielle climbed out of the car and squinted through the dusk at the man in front of her. With the wraparound sunglasses and chauffeur's cap gone, his narrow face and high forehead rendered him instantly recognisable. Not Bob Harvey. "Why are you doing this, Jim?"

The scars crisscrossing Jim Dembo's face twisted into a vicious mask. "Look at me. I'm a mess. My life is a mess. You and your family got off scot-free."

"Hardly. My mother *died* in the accident that did that to you." She gestured to the disfiguring marks. "I heard her final gasp while you were lying unconscious in the driver's seat." She struggled to breathe, the memory stabbing at an unhealed corner in her heart.

For a moment he looked uncertain. "Don't try to talk your way out of this," he snarled. "I know how your family operates. Plenty of promises to good ol' Jim and then not much more."

Jim had been well compensated. But no one knew better than she that money could never heal the trauma he'd suffered. "I'm so sorry for what happened to you. We were all victims of a drunk driver. It could've happened to anyone."

"You owe me! I've waited a long time for someone to pay."

Another man out to use her as a scapegoat. Danielle gritted her teeth against her angry response. But when he produced a gun, she stilled, her gaze fixed on the weapon like a snake on a snake charmer. Surely he didn't intend to kill her? Hadn't she read that kidnapped victims were more valuable alive than dead?

"Move!"

Frightened, Danielle scanned the surroundings. A short distance away a small wooden hut huddled in a thicket of *rimu* trees. Not the kind of place where she wanted to die. "Who owns this place? You?"

She wanted to keep him talking, to establish herself as a person in his eyes rather than a *thing* he could readily dispose of. But Jim didn't respond. Instead he grabbed her and shoved her forward.

Once inside the hut she blinked to accustom her eyes to the dim light. In a corner lay an old mattress topped with a heap of blankets. A collection of tools gleamed on shelves against the furthest wall. Screwdrivers, a hammer and an array of power tools. A first-aid box peeped out from under a coil of rope. On the lowest shelf there was a line of small empty glass bottles, the kind that roadside stalls used for honey and jam. The rest of the shelves were packed with tins of provisions, enough to feed a small army under siege. A burst of dismay filled her. Jim had planned this. She struggled to suppress the fear spewing against her innards. "Now what?"

"We wait."

\* \* \*

According to the luminous markings on Danielle's watch, forty hours had passed since Jim had snatched her. Chilled to the bone by the mountain air, she twisted restlessly on the lumpy, musty mattress. Earlier she'd had a bout of coughing that made her stomach heave. Jim had jerked her up, unlocked the door and thrust her out. He'd waited while she'd finished retching in the stand-alone toilet before leading her back inside.

It had to be nerves because she'd eaten nothing despite Jim's anger at her refusal. She didn't want food. She wanted Rico—the security of his arms. But Rico was on the other side of the world, taking care of his sick father, convinced that she was already instituting divorce proceedings.

Danielle shivered. Thinking about her circumstances was not helping. Eventually, in sheer desperation, she started talking. "What does your wife—Jenny, wasn't it?—think of what you're doing?

"My bloody wife left me!" Jim's violence made Danielle flinch. He punched a number into his cell phone and thrust it at her. "Here, you tell the bitch what's happening."

A sleepy female voice answered and Danielle asked, "Is that Jenny?"

"Who is this?" Danielle's heart sank at the suspicious anger in the other woman's voice. "My God, do you know what time it is?"

"It's important."

"It better be bloody critical."

Slowly, Danielle said, "Your husband made me call."

"My husband? You mean Jim? He's not my husband. I divorced him four months ago." A pause followed. Then, "What's he done? Is he in trouble?"

"Jenny, I need you to stay calm. My name's Danielle—"

With a curse Jim grabbed the phone and yelled wildly, "Jenny, I've kidnapped a woman. And I'm not going to release her until you agree to come back to me. If you keep refusing, I'm going to start cutting little bits off her and posting them to you—so you better come round fast."

Danielle heard the wail and the sobs that followed.

Jim snapped the phone off. "That'll teach the bitch."

Sick bastard! He wouldn't get his wife back like that. Danielle bit back the comment. Provoking him would serve no purpose—he was clearly out of control. Far better to come up with a plan to get herself out of this mess. In the dark outside she'd have a better chance to escape. Perhaps if she told him she needed the toilet…

Casually she picked up the jacket she'd taken off because it was tight and constricting, and slipped it on. She'd need all the warmth she could get out there in the hills.

"Next call." He sounded more confident, almost cocky. Shoving the phone into her hand, he said, "Dial your father. Tell him that I want two million dollars tomorrow night at six. Hand the phone to me so that I can give the location for the drop off. Make sure he knows that after six you lose a finger every hour, then your toes, then your ears, then your eyes. I'll send them to him in jars.

Danielle's gaze slid to the shelves. To the row of ominously empty jam jars, then to the power tools below. Her teeth started to clatter at the sight of the shiny skill saw. Even the first-aid box assumed a new menace. Nausea threatened again, and her stomach churned.

A metallic rasp sounded. She turned her head. Jim brandished the gun. "Make sure he understands I'm serious. You won't have long to talk, because I'm not giving the bastards the chance to get a trace on me. If you tell him who I am or where you think you might be, I'll shoot you, understand?"

Dumbly she nodded, her head spinning from the instructions, the horror of what he planned to do.

"Okay, now phone."

She dialled the familiar number, praying that her father would be in. Two, three, four rings. *Come on, Daddy.* Five. Six. Her shoulders drooped as she waited for the answer service to kick in. The click of the handset being lifted was music to her ears. She felt breathless with relief.

"Hello?" a familiar voice said.

"Rico…?" she gasped out. *He was back!*

"Danielle, where you are?" Rico's voice rang with urgency.

Danielle hesitated, glanced sideways. Jim raised the gun, the round dark hole at the end of the barrel staring at her. Fear, corrosive and sharp burned her throat.

"I don't know," she choked out.

"You're being threatened!"

"Yes," she confirmed, and gave Jim a conciliatory smile.

Jim grabbed the phone from her, and her gut-wrenching despair shocked her. She needed to hear Rico's voice, to draw strength from him.

Jim held the cell phone away from her and she could hear Rico saying something. Then Jim thrust it back into her hand. "I didn't expect D'Alessio. Make it convincing, make him fear for your safety." He waved to the tools. "I'll call him six o'clock tomorrow evening with details of the drop. If he doesn't have the cash, the carving begins." He smiled, a sad smile that made her turn cold with apprehension. "Oh—and remind him how much you love him—give him an incentive to raise the money from your father."

He obviously didn't know that Rico was wealthy in his own right. Had Jim made any other slips? Before she could think further, Rico's voice, dark and dangerous, called her name.

"I'm here," she said softly, and repeated the information Jim had relayed to her.

Rico said rapidly. "Now listen to me. Guard your responses, but I need all the help I can get. Do you know this man?"

"Yes." Desperately she tried to think of a way to give Rico a clue without endangering herself. Nothing brilliant came to mind. With time running away, she simply said, "Oh, Rico. I'm so sorry to hear your father's ill, I haven't seen him since he went to hospital, after your mother died."

*Please God, let him work it out.* That she was talking about *her* mother's death and that the man she'd not seen since he went to hospital was Jim.

Jim shook her shoulder. "That's enough social chitchat. Tell him you love him. Blow some kisses."

Oh, God!

She wanted to rail against Jim, tell him to go to hell. Instead she compressed her lips and remained stubbornly mute. The gun appeared again, dancing past her nose, and her eyes stretched wide.

*So what if Rico knew?*

It was only the truth after all.

"I love you," she said flatly into the phone.

Silence met her statement. A silence so darkly intimidating that her knees folded, and she started to tremble. Small infinitely painful quivers that turned to shakes as she waited for Rico to say something.

At last he broke the stillness. "He made you say that, didn't he?" His voice was low and hard, relentless.

She nodded, then remembered he couldn't see her. "Yes," she muttered, trying to stop her teeth from chattering.

Jim grabbed the phone. Holding it away, he snarled, "You little bitch! I want more passion. I need Rico to get your father to send that money. Get some life into the show." His eyes lit up. "I know. Tell him you're pregnant."

A broken laugh burst from her. "Believe me, I'm soooh *not* pregnant."

"He doesn't know that." Shoving the phone at her, he said, "Do it!"

"Danielle!"

She heard Rico's wild yell and said quickly, "I'm here. I'm here. There's something I need to tell you."

"I'm waiting."

"I'm—" She squeezed her eyes shut as her chest closed like a vise around her heart, but the terrible ache grew worse.

"Danielle, what the hell's the matter?" Rico's voice held a depth of panic she'd never heard. "Has that bastard…hurt you?"

"I'm fine." She gave a broken laugh. "Actually, I'm not. I'm tired and sore right now." Jim swung the gun and the butt connected against the side of her head. She flinched, biting back a moan of pain. His hand lifted again. Hurriedly she added, "And I'm pregnant."

Her stark words rushed into a void. Suddenly the nausea, the dislike of coffee, the lack of appetite all made sense. Despite her surroundings, the threat Jim posed, her heart soared.

She *was* pregnant.

It was true. The impossible had happened.

Then, when she thought she'd scream from the force of the tension buzzing inside her head, Rico said with dangerous softness, "Run that by me again."

"I'm pregnant," she repeated softly.

"He couldn't have found a better way to torture you, could he?" Rico's curt voice penetrated the haze that enveloped her. "Tell that cruel bastard that I'm going to track him down, and when I find him I'm going to deal with him." The white-hot rage made her cringe. "And he'd better not lay a finger on you, because I'll take him apart with my bare hands."

Not even the droning noise of the helicopter and the knowledge that he'd rescued countless kidnap victims could stifle Rico's anxiety as they flew through the night, the blades tuk-tukking outside. Ignoring the team of hostage negotiators and Ken Pascal's silent presence was easy, the hard part was dealing with the quaver he'd heard in Danielle's voice when the call had finally come. She'd been so brave, giving him the clue he needed to figure out the identity of her kidnapper.

He prayed that she was safe. Ruthlessly he quashed his fear that she might die tonight, that he wouldn't be able to save her. Just like he'd failed Lucia…and Danielle's mother. *Nothing was going to happen to her.*

His Princess. Would she ever forgive him? Blindly he stared at his combat boots sticking out in front of him. Hell. His mouth tightened. He'd certainly put every possible foot wrong with Danielle.

He'd been so dumb. Criminally dumb. The fear that had snared him like barbed wire when he'd learned she'd been kidnapped had frozen his ability to think, stopping him from realising why he hurt so damn much. Three words. *I love you.* That was all it had taken. Three words uttered in her dull, flat voice for him to realise why he ached, why he could barely think straight.

And why the drive for revenge against the Sinclair family no longer provided a goal for him to focus on. To have another chance with Danielle, he'd gladly forfeit his grandiose scheme.

He'd give up everything.

Even his dream of a child.

But she didn't know that. Danielle was convinced he

wanted the divorce she'd offered. To think he'd placed his duty to his family ahead of the woman he…cared…for. If only he could start over…react differently to her revelation that she couldn't have a child. And offer sympathy and support for the suffering she'd endured.

*I'm pregnant.* He swallowed, his throat tight and dry. The words must've cracked her heart. They'd torn his apart. Suddenly easing her pain had become more important to him than anything in his world, and revenge, the drive for a son to pass the D'Alessio name to, were no longer his sole obsession.

Somehow Danielle had become that.


"Jim," Danielle called through the murk to the figure slouching in the decrepit chair beside the door. The only light came from a flickering gas lamp. "I need the toilet."

"Huh?" She'd woken him. He sounded disorientated.

"I need to go to the toilet. Now." She'd waited deliberately, waited until it was dark and very late so that he wouldn't be so vigilant. She injected a note of desperation into her voice. "Please hurry, Jim."

Cursing, he stumbled over to where she lay trussed like a turkey. He yanked her to her feet, "Come on, then."

"It's dark outside. I'll fall on the uneven ground. Can't you untie my legs?"

"Why should I care if you fall?"

"At the moment I'm worth two million dollars to you, surely you should take some care of your cash cow?" she asked, snippy and tired.

Without a word he bent and tugged the leg ropes free. Danielle held out her wrists. "These too, please otherwise I can't—" She stopped, embarrassed at the hygiene details. But he muttered impatiently and untied her hands.

"Thank you, Jim. I won't be long."

"Hey, you're not going out there alone. I'm coming, too."

"Where am I going to go?" she retorted. "I don't even know where we are. The last thing I need is to get lost in the hills."

But Jim was already pulling on his boots and unbolting the door. The instant the door opened, she slipped through. His hand closed on her sleeve, pulling her back, "Not so fast."

Then she heard it. The drone of a helicopter. A rush of blood made her head spin. This was it, her chance. A swift glance upward showed nothing but blackness, and she sagged. Had it already passed overhead?

Jim had heard it, too. "Bugger! Get back," he snapped.

She hesitated. If she obeyed him it would all be over. Danielle aimed a swift kick at the gas lamp just inside the door. There was an instant of darkness as it tumbled, macabre shadows dancing across the walls, and then the flames leaped as the sacks and blankets caught fire.

She wrestled with Jim to free herself. *Please God, let them see it.* A bush fire was always cause to investigate.

"Bitch!" he grunted, as her knee caught a sensitive spot. Fired by fear and desperation she fought and kicked like never before. He grabbed at her and she slipped off her jacket so that he was left holding nothing but the garment. She burst out the door into the night, her face upturned as she searched the dark sky.

The helicopter was overhead now. She could feel the beat of the wind on her face. The searchlights came on and she waved and yelled. The next instant the night was swarming with dark figures. A figure swooped like some enormous bird of prey, and she shrank back.

"Danielle!"

At the familiar voice, her knees gave out. She stumbled. "Rico?" she whispered in disbelief. Then his arms were around her, tight and hard, and the familiar sensation of warmth and security washed over her.

She should've known she could rely on Rico to find her! She caught a brief glimpse of Jim surrounded by a cluster of camouflage-clad men, his arms pinned behind his back, then she closed her eyes and concentrated on the roughness of Rico's cheek against hers, the silkiness of his hair against her brow.

*"Dio!"* he rasped. "Never *dare* put me through that again."

"You're insane if you think I want a repeat performance," she murmured, soaking in the raw, masculine scent of him. "All I want is…" *You,* she almost uttered. Instead she said prosaically, "…is a hot bath and a clean bed."

"And a meal."

"No, I'm not hungry." The thought of food turned her stomach, and a small, secret smile slid over her face. She'd tell Rico about her suspicions soon enough.

"This has been the worst time of my life. I've aged decades knowing you were in that bastard's hands."

She slid her arms around his neck and pressed her body up against the hard warmth of his. "It's over, Rico."

His finger tilted her chin up, and her heartbeat quickened. But the kiss was gentle rather than sensual, a wealth of tenderness in the brief caress.

"It *is* over. You've had a hellish time. Home for you, I think."

"Please, Rico." She stopped. "Oh, I nearly forgot in this rumpus, is Tymon…okay?"

"Apart from a slight concussion he's fine. Jim knew how Ken Pascal works, and your father's security arrangements have changed little in years. That's how he could get into the house and your bedroom. He's still kept in touch with Bob, they're hunting buddies, so it was easy for him to find out what was happening, and to turn up early when a new driver was assigned. Too easy. I'm going to go over the security with Ken, toughen it up."

"Bob Harvey was…involved?"

"No, but he's chastened. Believe me, he'll never look at you with anything except respect in his eyes." His voice was hard.

Danielle dropped her head in her hands. "I can't believe that the horror of the last few months is finally over. It's been awful—horrible! At last I can get on with my life, get out from under the shadow that I've been living in. I want my life back."

He tensed and put her away from him, and she wanted to cry at the chill that crept through her.

"Yes," he agreed. "The sooner we get your life back to normal, the better."

The sound of the phone ringing woke Danielle the following morning. She waited for an instant, then rolled over and half sat up. A hollow remained where Rico had slept. She made a moan of disappointment and reached for the telephone.

"Danielle!" At Kim's wail she groaned, ill prepared for her sister's dramatics. "I thought you were going to die. I need to tell you that I don't want you to die, that I'm sorry."

A sensation akin to déjà vu swept over her. She braced herself for Kim's latest revelation. "I'm fine. I just need a good rest. Perhaps you, Bradley and Dad can visit tomorrow?"

But Kim barely paused before she was off, chattering hard. "I've always been jealous of you. Everyone liked you. The teachers, the girls at school, their parents—I wanted to be just like you."

Stunned, Danielle said, "Kim, you're bright, vibrant and beautiful. Your own person. You don't need to be me."

"I've finally realised that. Bradley taught me. Funny, really, because for years the *only* reason I've wanted Bradley was because I thought you wanted him. Now I don't know how I ever *lived* without him."

That sounded like how she felt about Rico. Danielle's brain slowed, "Kim, why did you try to seduce Rico years ago?"

Kim didn't utter a word.

Feeling her way, Danielle asked, "Was it because you thought I fancied him? After all, it was the night after—" She stopped, unable to say more.

"Yes." It was barely a whisper. "I *wanted* to sleep with him and tell you I had done it. But he chased me away. Then Daddy caught me coming out of his room and it all went horribly wrong. Rico told Daddy that he should find me a nice boy to date, and shut the door in our faces. I didn't know what to say. Daddy was furious. And I was scared. So I told him that Rico had forced me—just a little. The next thing the police were there and a policewoman was taking my statement." A pause followed. "I didn't know how to undo it. And you…you'd gone all silent and withdrawn again, and I felt too guilty to talk to you."

"Oh, Kim-ber-ly! You should've confided in me. Haven't I always sorted your problems out?"

"I didn't think you'd help me that time. You never saw your face when you watched Rico. You used to moon over him. I *hated* him. I *knew* you were going to end up hurt. So I wanted to put you off him for life."

"You thought if you slept with him, I'd hate him?" Danielle was shocked. "You were too young for those kind of games, Kim."

"No one cared what I did. And I told you, I didn't like the way you watched him."

Her sister had been jealous of the attention she'd paid Rico but in some weird way Kim had been trying to protect her. But with what disastrous results.

"Is it all fixed between you guys now? Daddy says he thought Rico was going to smash walls yesterday."

At the image Danielle almost smiled. "Kim, you've got a husband now, one who loves you. Work on keeping it that way. You've apologised to me and you can apologise to Rico tomorrow."

"Okay," she said amenably.

Danielle set the handset down and stepped out of bed. She pulled on the lacy robe that hung over the bed end. She wanted Rico, needed the heat of his arms around her. Filled with lazy languor, she made for the door.

She was still smiling as she made her way down the stairs, wondering at how much Kim had matured since discovering she loved Bradley. No doubt her sister would have another hundred questions when she and Bradley arrived tomorrow.

The sight of a suitcase and a bag standing beside the front door wiped the smile off her face and brought her to an abrupt halt. Danielle told herself that the luggage must belong to Tymon, he must've called to say he was on his way to collect it.

When Rico appeared from the kitchen, she anxiously scanned his features. His face was expressionless, and then she knew.

"You're going?"

He nodded.

"Why?"

"You need to put all this behind you. I'll only be a daily reminder."

Her hand rested on her stomach. She had a daily reminder already. But Rico didn't know that.

Then he said, "It never occurred to me to wonder why the only clause you insisted on putting in that infernal contract we signed—apart from the demand that I leave Kim alone—was that I would vacate your house when you asked. I should've known then that there would be no child. You'd never have given up the rights to your child. *Never!* So I'm not going to wait for you to boot me out."

Danielle sighed. He was going to make this difficult. It was going to take time for him to forgive her, to trust her again. But she had a whole lifetime to wait. "Where are you going? Back to Italy?"

"Perhaps."

Her heart ached at the thought of an ocean separating them. Did he mean never to return? But she hid her fear. "I suppose your family needs you."

"My father is already much better. We've been in contact. He and my mother send their regards, so does Bella."

She wasn't going to make it easy for him to walk away. "I was looking forward to meeting them."

He ignored her comment. Instead he said, "My plans aren't final yet. Even if I visit my family it will only be for a little while. I like it here. New Zealand is where I want to spend my life."

Relief swept her. She tried—and failed—to decipher some hidden meaning in his words. Did that mean he intended to keep in touch with her? She opened her mouth to ask, but the words that she uttered were a world apart from what she'd meant to say. "I think I'm really pregnant," she said baldly.

There was an instant of complete silence.

*"The hell you are!"*

He was across the space separating them in two long strides. He lifted his hands. She waited for him to sweep her up in a hug. It never came, instead his hands dropped awkwardly to his sides.

"I'm not dead certain, but I'm pretty sure I am." When she

realised how absurd that sounded, she went quiet and simply stared at him with wide eyes, waiting for his next move.

"How did it happen?"

"Er…" She stopped. Her mouth softened. "You know more about the how than I ever did. I can't believe you're asking."

"I know *how*. I meant how *could* it have happened?"

"After the accident they had to remove my spleen, and one ovary was badly mangled. The other ovary took a bashing, too. I spent hours in surgery and they managed to save both. But the doctors told me and Daddy that there was little chance of a baby because of all the scarring on the fallopian tubes."

Rico didn't say a word.

She rushed into speech. "I can't promise you a boy. Or that there'll ever be another child. With my medical history if I'm pregnant, it's already a miracle."

"Do you really think it matters to me whether you're carrying a boy or a girl?" His face held a strange expression.

She spread her hands. "I thought you'd want a boy to carry the D'Alessio family name, you being the last of the line and all that. Heck, I shouldn't be telling you anything. I first wanted to go for a test, confirm it. Perhaps I'll even have to stay in bed for a long time." She shrugged her shoulders. "I'm talking too fast—I'm overwhelmed."

"You're not alone." At last his hands rested on her shoulders. "But what I was trying to say was that it doesn't matter if it's a boy or girl. Simply knowing you're pregnant—"

"What do you mean?"

He was pale, his face grim. "I don't think I can walk away. However much I think it's the right thing for me to do."

"*The right thing to do?* How can you even think that?"

"It's a life sentence, you realise that, don't you? I'm too Catholic to ever consider—"

"—abortion? Are you mad? This may be my only chance—"

"I was going to say divorce but that's not an option now there's a child involved." The hands on her shoulders looped around her neck. He gave a soft tug.

She resisted. "Who said anything about divorce?" she challenged.

"You did—you said you wanted to get on with your life. That's why I was leaving, to give you space until you decided what you wanted. But I can't walk away from my child."

She wanted him to love *her.* Truly, deeply, madly.

Like she loved him.

But that didn't mean he could walk all over her. "I'm not giving the baby up," she said, setting her jaw and squaring her shoulders.

"I know that. I'm not a monster." His fingers stroked the soft skin of her nape under her hair. The familiar warmth winnowed over her skin. She wanted to throw herself into his arms, to take him on any terms she could have him.

But she wasn't telling him that. Yet. "But the contract said I'd give the baby up to you."

His gaze was very direct. "We both know you never had any intention of falling pregnant, so how could you have intended to give up your child…and fulfil the contract?"

She simply shrugged.

"I'm not going to take your child."

"What about being the last of the D'Alessio line?"

"It doesn't matter. I can't take the baby from you." His voice was incredibly gentle. "Danielle—"

But she'd started to hope again. He must love her! Why else would he walk away, but stay near? She raised her eyes. "Yes?" she whispered, suddenly terrified of being wrong.

"I no longer crave revenge. All I want is your love. And a baby would be a miracle to seal it." His eyes were dark and vulnerable. "But a child is not essential to my happiness. Your love, however, is essential."

"Oh, Rico! Don't you know you've got it?"

"I need to hear you say it again."

Confused, she asked, "Again?"

"The last time I heard you say it I thought the pain would never go away. I wanted to hold you, kiss you. But I had to rescue you before I could do it."

*The ransom call!* Her face cleared. "You didn't think I meant it, did you?"

"No. I knew Jim had forced you to say it, to up the stakes. But I discovered, more than anything in the world, I wanted to hear you say it one day with meaning. For it to be true."

"Rico," she lifted her face to his, like a flower searching for the morning sun, and said, "I'll always love you. I thought you'd never forgive my deception."

*"Dio."* His eyes were velvet-dark with the intensity of his emotions. "I gave you little choice. I was so focused on revenge I'm not surprised you tried to give me my comeuppance. I behaved abominably. I deserved everything you dished out!" He drew her close. "I love you. How did I ever get so lucky?"

His arms tightened around her. The kiss that he gave her was gentle, nurturing, promising that he'd never leave her, that he'd always be by her side, to guard her from any fear and uncertainty.

As they came up for air, Danielle said slowly, "I think I'm the lucky one." And then leaned forward to concentrate on matching the kisses the man she loved more than life was pressing against her lips.

Slowly the familiar pounding started to pulse through her, and she murmured against his mouth, "I told Kim I needed rest, perhaps it's time to go up?"

"How I love you, Princess." For an instant, deep wonderment glittered in his eyes, then he laughed. "In fact, I believe we're both about to get lucky," Rico said, then swept her into his arms and headed for the stairs.

# Epilogue

"I've brought you a present."

"Another one?" Danielle rose clumsily from where she'd been kneeling to pot seedlings for the coming summer as Rico burst through the sliding door. The familiar joy at the sight of him caused her heart to skip a beat.

He frowned in concern. "You should've waited for me to help you with that."

"I wanted to get the plants in." But her back ached with the heaviness caused by the last month of her pregnancy. "The baby and I are fine."

Rico had been stubborn in his refusal to allow the doctor to reveal the sex of the baby. Danielle couldn't help worrying about how he'd react if the baby turned out to be the girl she suspected lay within her womb…rather than the boy Rico's father desired. And they both knew this might be the only child they'd ever be blessed with. A miracle of their love.

Umberto and Bianca would be arriving in six weeks. Months ago Danielle had flown to Italy with Rico to meet his parents, and they were ecstatic about the baby's imminent arrival. Her father had been unexpectedly pleased, too—doubly so, with the news that Kim was also expecting a baby.

"Aren't you going to open it?"

She reached for the package, wondering what he'd bought her this time. "You spoil me to death, do you know that?"

"Not to death—I celebrate your life, my love. I love you."

Her heart turned over at the intensity in his eyes, the passion in his voice. "I know. And I love you, too."

He moved to stand behind her, and wrapped his arms around her. "Happy?"

She rested against him, drawing on his immense strength while she clutched the brightly wrapped gift. "Every day of my life."

She spoke the truth. Life with Rico had brought her love and a sense of security that she'd never known. Totally in control of his environment, Rico had even managed to get Jim Dembo's kidnapping sentence reduced to a year's imprisonment followed by intense counselling and community service. Danielle had been relieved. She'd been granted a second shot at happiness with Rico—and she'd also reestablished a relationship with her father. Jim deserved another chance, too.

"Good." He gave her stomach a pat and stepped back. "Now open the gift."

She tore the wrapping away to reveal a box. Slowly she removed the lid. "Annabelle!" Her throat tightened and tears pricked. "It *is* Annabelle, isn't it?" The doll wore a dress almost identical in style and colour.

"Yes. I searched until I found someone who could restore her. But she looks a little different. No one can survive what she did without some changes."

"She's beautiful." The doll's lips were rosier, her smile more natural, less coy. "She looks happy." Danielle hugged Annabelle close, catching a faint hint of the scent that had always reminded her of her mother.

"Thank you, Rico."

"My pleasure."

She tried to explain. "She's more than a doll. My mother gave her to me. She told me every girl should have a special baby. Annabelle was mine." Below her heart her unborn daughter shifted. Danielle rubbed her stomach and the baby quietened. *Their special baby.*

"I knew how you felt about Annabelle—I couldn't dispose of her. I couldn't give you your mother back, but I could give you Annabelle. And…if you want…one day soon we can go look for a doll for our daughter. A piece of us she can keep forever."

*Our daughter.*

Rico knew! Everything was going to be all right. She smiled at him, absorbing Rico's love and the sunshine of the morning. "She'll like that."

\* \* \* \* \*

*Look for THE KYRIAKOS VIRGIN BRIDE*
*by Tessa Radley,*
*the first book in the BILLIONAIRE HEIRS miniseries*
*from Silhouette Desire*
*on sale September 2007*

THE ROYAL HOUSE OF NIROLI
*Always passionate, always proud*

The richest royal family in the world—united by blood and
passion, torn apart by deceit and desire

Nestled in the azure blue of the Mediterranean Sea, the majestic
island of Niroli has prospered for centuries. The Fierezza men
have worn the crown with passion and pride since ancient
times. But now, as the king's health declines, and his two sons
have been tragically killed, the crown is in jeopardy.

The clock is ticking—a new heir must be found before the
king is forced to abdicate. By royal decree the internationally
scattered members of the Fierezza family are summoned to
claim their destiny. But any person who takes the throne must
do so according to The Rules of the Royal House of Niroli.
Soon secrets and rivalries emerge as the descendents of this
ancient royal line vie for position and power. Only a true
Fierezza can become ruler—a person dedicated to their
country, their people…and their eternal love!

*Each month starting in July 2007,*
*Harlequin Presents is delighted to bring you*
*an exciting installment from*
THE ROYAL HOUSE OF NIROLI,
*in which you can follow the epic search*
*for the true Nirolian king.*
*Eight heirs, eight romances, eight fantastic stories!*

Here's your chance to enjoy a sneak preview of the first
book delivered to you by royal decree…

FIVE minutes later she was standing immobile in front of the study's window, her original purpose of coming in forgotten, as she stared in shocked horror at the envelope she was holding. Waves of heat followed by icy chill surged through her body. She could hardly see the address now through her blurred vision, but the crest on its left-hand front corner stood out, its *royal* crest, followed by the address: *HRH Prince Marco of Niroli...*

She didn't hear Marco's key in the apartment door, she didn't even hear him calling out her name. Her shock was so great that nothing could penetrate it. It encased her in a kind of bubble, which only concentrated the torment of what she was suffering and branded it on her brain so that it could never be forgotten. It was only finally pierced by the sudden opening of the study door as Marco walked in.

"Welcome home, *Your Highness*. I suppose I ought to curtsy." She waited, praying that he would laugh and tell her that she had got it all wrong, that the envelope she was holding, addressing him as Prince Marco of Niroli, was some silly mistake. But like a tiny candle flame shivering vulnerably in the dark, her hope trembled fearfully. And then the look in Marco's eyes extinguished it as cruelly as a hand placed callously over a dying person's face to stem their last breath.

"Give that to me," he demanded, taking the envelope from her.

"It's too late, Marco," Emily told him brokenly. "I know the truth now…." She dug her teeth in her lower lip to try to force back her own pain.

"You had no right to go through my desk," Marco shot back at her furiously, full of loathing at being caught off-guard and forced into a position in which he was in the wrong, making him determined to find something he could accuse Emily of. "I trusted you…."

Emily could hardly believe what she was hearing. "No, you didn't trust me, Marco, and you didn't trust me because you knew that I couldn't trust you. And you knew that because you're a liar, and liars don't trust people because they know that they themselves cannot be trusted." She not only felt sick, she also felt as though she could hardly breathe. "You are Prince Marco of Niroli…. How could you not tell me who you are and still live with me as intimately as we have lived together?" she demanded brokenly.

"Stop being so ridiculously dramatic," Marco demanded fiercely. "You are making too much of the situation."

"*Too much?*" Emily almost screamed the words at him. "When were you going to tell me, Marco? Perhaps you just planned to walk away without telling me anything? After all, what do my feelings matter to you?"

"Of course they matter." Marco stopped her sharply. "And it was in part to protect them, and you, that I decided not to inform you when my grandfather first announced that he intended to step down from the throne and hand it on to me."

"To protect me?" Emily nearly choked on her fury. "Hand

on the throne? No wonder you told me when you first took me to bed that all you wanted was sex. You *knew* that was the only kind of relationship there could ever be between us! You *knew* that one day you would be Niroli's king. No doubt you are expected to marry a princess. Is she picked out for you already, your *royal* bride?"

\* \* \* \* \*

*Look for THE FUTURE KING'S PREGNANT MISTRESS*
*by Penny Jordan in July 2007,*
*from Harlequin Presents,*
*available wherever books are sold.*

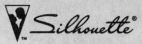

## Silhouette®

### Romantic
# SUSPENSE

*Sparked by Danger,*
*Fueled by Passion.*

---

### *Mission: Impassioned*

A brand-new miniseries begins with

# *My Spy*

### By *USA TODAY* bestselling author

# Marie Ferrarella

She had to trust him with her life....
It was the most daring mission of Joshua Lazlo's
career: rescuing the prime minister of England's
daughter from a gang of cold-blooded kidnappers.
But nothing prepared the shadowy secret agent
for a fiery woman whose touch ignited something
far more dangerous.

# *My Spy*

#### #1472

*Available July 2007 wherever you buy books!*

---

# nocturne™

## DON'T MISS THE RIVETING CONCLUSION TO THE RAINTREE TRILOGY

# RAINTREE: SANCTUARY

by *New York Times* bestselling author

# BEVERLY BARTON

Mercy, guardian of the Raintree
homeplace, takes a stand against
the Ansara wizards to battle for
the Clan's future.

*On sale July,*
*wherever books are sold.*

# COMING NEXT MONTH

### #1807 THE CEO'S SCANDALOUS AFFAIR—
**Roxanne St. Claire**
*Dynasties: The Garrisons*
He needed her for just one night—but the repercussions of their
sensual evening could last a lifetime!

### #1808 HIGH-SOCIETY MISTRESS—Katherine Garbera
*The Mistresses*
He will stop at nothing to take over his business rival's
company…including bedding his enemy's daughter and making
her his mistress.

### #1809 MARRIED TO HIS BUSINESS—Elizabeth Bevarly
*Millionaire of the Month*
To get his assistant back this CEO plans to woo and seduce her.
But he isn't prepared when she ups the stakes on *his* game.

### #1810 THE PRINCE'S ULTIMATE DECEPTION—
**Emilie Rose**
*Monte Carlo Affairs*
It was a carefree vacation romance. Until she discovers she's
having an affair with a prince in disguise.

### #1811 ROSSELLINI'S REVENGE AFFAIR—
**Yvonne Lindsay**
He blamed her for his family's misery and sought revenge in a
most passionate way!

### #1812 THE BOSS'S DEMAND—Jennifer Lewis
She was pregnant with the boss's baby—but wanted more than
just the convenient marriage he was offering.

SDCNM0607